Rotten

Saekisan

ILLUSTRATION BY
Hanekoto

Amane Fujimiya

Itsuki Akazawa

©Hanekoto

Mahiru Shiina

Chitose Shirakawa

He crouched down and gazed at Mahiru,
who was letting out extremely adorable
soft little snores as she slumbered.

*...She's too defenseless—
what do I do?*

©Hanekoto

Contents

Amane Fujimiya

A first-year high school student who began
living alone shortly after the start of the school
year. He is poor at every type of housework
and leads a self-indulgent life. He tends to put
himself down, but he's a very kind soul at heart.

Mahiru Shiina

A classmate who lives next door to
Amane. She is the most beautiful girl in
school and is often called an angel by her
peers. After seeing Amane's atrocious
lifestyle, she winds up cooking for him.

The Angel Next Door Spoils Me Rotten

2

Saekisan

ILLUSTRATION BY
Hanekoto

NEW YORK

The Angel Next Door Spoils Me Rotten 2

Saekisan

TRANSLATION BY NICOLE WILDER ✶ COVER ART BY HANEKOTO

OTONARI NO TENSHISAMA NI ITSUNOMANIKA DAMENINGEN NI SARETEITA KEN Vol. 2
Copyright © 2020 Saekisan
Illustration © 2020 Hanekoto
All rights reserved.
Original Japanese edition published in 2020 by SB Creative Corp.
This English edition is published by arrangement with SB Creative Corp., Tokyo in care of Tuttle-Mori Agency, Inc., Tokyo.

English translation © 2021 by Yen Press, LLC

Yen On
150 West 30th Street, 19th Floor
New York, NY 10001

Visit us at yenpress.com ✶ facebook.com/yenpress ✶ twitter.com/yenpress
yenpress.tumblr.com ✶ instagram.com/yenpress

First Yen On Edition: August 2021

Yen On is an imprint of Yen Press, LLC.
The Yen On name and logo are trademarks of Yen Press, LLC.

The publisher is not responsible for websites (or their content)
that are not owned by the publisher.

Library of Congress Cataloging-in-Publication Data
Names: Saekisan, author. | Hanekoto, illustrator. | Wilder, Nicole. translator.
Title: The angel next door spoils me rotten / Saekisan ; illustration by Hanekoto ; translation by Nicole Wilder.
Other titles: Otonari no tenshi-sama ni Itsu no ma ni ka dame ningen ni sareteita ken. English
Description: First Yen On edition. | New York : Yen On, 2020- |
Identifiers: LCCN 2020043583 | ISBN 9781975319236 (v. 1 ; trade paperback) | ISBN 9781975322694 (v. 2 ; trade paperback)
Subjects: CYAC: Love—Fiction.
Classification: LCC PZ7.1.S2413 An 2020 | DDC [Fic]—dc23
LC record available at https://lccn.loc.gov/2020043583

ISBNs: 978-1-9753-2269-4 (paperback)
978-1-9753-2270-0 (ebook)

1 3 5 7 9 10 8 6 4 2

LSC-C

Printed in the United States of America

Chapter 1

Spending the End of the Year with the Angel

Once Christmas had passed, the whole world could feel the end of the year approaching.

The day after spending Christmas with Mahiru, Amane went out to do a bit of shopping on his own. By the time he was finished, his surroundings had undergone a dramatic shift, and Amane admired the new scenery on his way home.

The lights strung up around the city remained, but the ornamented trees and Christmas decorations had already been replaced with more traditional Japanese adornments. The shops had also updated their merchandise, selling New Year's decorations and foods. If there were any Christmas things still in stock, at best they had been reduced in price and were displayed under INVENTORY CLEAR-OUT SALE labels.

Amane nestled his face deeper into the billowy folds of his scarf as he pondered the sudden changeover. Mahiru had given him the monochrome houndstooth-patterned scarf as a Christmas present. It was both practical and tasteful; it looked stylish and felt very nice to the touch, and most importantly, it kept the chilly winter winds at bay.

Amane had never really worn a scarf before, so he was feeling grateful for this one as he checked over the contents of the shopping bags hanging from his arms.

Though the two of them were supposed to share this responsibility—in order to reduce the burden on Mahiru, who did all the cooking—Amane usually went out to buy the ingredients, armed with a shopping list.

It was a cold day, and Amane's bags were stuffed with vegetables and mushrooms and meat—Mahiru must have been planning to make a hot pot. The plentiful vegetables were her way of wordlessly insisting that Amane eat a more balanced, nutritious diet.

He laughed quietly to himself, amused that Mahiru was somehow still looking out for him even when she wasn't actually present.

He checked again to be sure that he'd gotten everything, then quickly returned home, shivering against the relentless cold.

"Welcome back."

It was already evening when Amane entered his apartment, and Mahiru was there to greet him.

It was kind of a strange feeling, being welcomed into his own apartment, but recently he had gotten used to it.

"Mm, I'm back... I bought some thinly sliced mochi; I hope that's okay?"

"You want to cook it in the hot pot, right?"

"Yeah. I also got some ramen to finish off the meal."

"...There's no way I can eat that much, you know."

"Don't worry, I'll make sure it doesn't go to waste."

Amane had never been the type to eat huge meals before, but now, thanks to Mahiru's cooking, he had started enjoying more sizable dinners. In fact, he found his new portion sizes a bit concerning and had resolved to start weight training.

Mahiru seemed to be watching her diet as well. She rarely

prepared any fattening foods. On the other hand, she also seemed to think that Amane could stand to put on a bit of weight, since he was so slim. Amane hoped he would add muscle and not fat.

"Well, if you're going to finish it, then that's fine. Here, give me the bags. I'll put the things in the fridge. You go wash your hands."

"I know, I know."

Amane handed the full shopping bags to Mahiru and obediently headed for the sink.

"Come to think of it, what are you doing for New Year's, Mahiru?"

After finishing every last bite of the day's delicious meal, as always, Amane suddenly asked Mahiru the question that had been weighing on his mind.

"New Year's... Well, there's no point in going home, so I'll be here."

He realized his blunder when he heard her indifferent tone, but Mahiru didn't actually seem all that bothered.

Her relationship with her parents wasn't good, so she always had a cold attitude whenever the conversation turned to her family.

But if that's the case, won't Mahiru be spending the holiday alone?

Amane had his standing promise to show his face at home once every six months, so he had been planning to visit during the long break—that was before he had met Mahiru.

"You're going back home, right, Amane?"

"That's right; I'm pretty much under orders to show up."

He glanced over at her and saw that the expression in her eyes was somewhat chillier than usual. She seemed to have resolved herself to spending the holiday alone, what with Amane going away and all.

"...Man, when I get home, I'm gonna get absolutely grilled about you."

"How terrible…"

"I can probably get by with just giving my dad the basics, but my mom is going to want to hear a whole lot more."

"That's awfully strange, since I talk to her all the time."

"You really got familiar with my mom in no time…"

For some reason, Mahiru had made fast friends with Amane's mother and, without him noticing, had been sending her photos and private stories…which frankly killed him a little inside. But Mahiru obviously enjoyed it, so Amane didn't see any harm in it. He only hoped she wasn't telling his mother anything more than she absolutely needed to know.

Recalling the distant, lonely expression that crossed Mahiru's face from time to time, Amane decided that he didn't want to leave her here alone.

"Well, I did just see Mom a little while ago… I would miss seeing Dad, but I wonder if it would be all right if I didn't go home for the New Year… Besides, I'm supposed to go back during spring vacation anyway."

Amane was thinking that if he stayed here for the holiday, they could continue having dinner together like always…that is, if it wasn't too much of an imposition on Mahiru.

"…Oh?"

"Mm. Plus, I want to eat your New Year's noodles."

"What a glutton you are."

"It's all because of your cooking."

"…Even when it's ready-made?"

"That's right."

Even if she only boiled the prepackaged soba noodles, Amane was sure he would still enjoy them. Because the important thing about their shared meals was the time they spent together.

"…You're an awfully strange person," Mahiru remarked.

"Oh, hush."

He saw her smile slightly.

"…Thank you."

"What for?"

"For whatever."

Mahiru didn't say anything further, but her expression brightened somewhat, and she squeezed her favorite cushion.

And then December 31 arrived. New Year's Eve was bringing the year to a close. For many, it was a busy day, spent cleaning and preparing for the year to come, but—

"Um, hey, Mahiru?"

"What is it?"

"…Are you sure you don't want me to help with anything?"

From his position sitting comfortably on the living room couch, Amane was gazing at Mahiru's back as she was standing apron-clad in his kitchen. She had been in there since that morning, making *osechi*, the traditional fare for the New Year holiday.

Since they had decided to ring in the New Year together, naturally they needed enough to feed two.

Amane had assumed they would be purchasing it premade, but apparently Mahiru intended to make it all by hand. That would have been quite a task even for a skilled homemaker, so it was surprising for even this brilliant high school girl to tackle it all alone.

Amane was seriously impressed, but Mahiru had said, "Well, there's no way we can get *osechi* from a store now. You have to order it well in advance."

Admittedly, she was absolutely right, but even so, Amane admired Mahiru for deciding to make everything herself.

Of course, she took shortcuts where she could. For instance, boiling their own black soybeans would be very time-consuming and keep one burner occupied for far too long, so they had bought some prepared soybeans instead.

"Amane, you seem uncomfortable whenever I say you don't have to do anything, but do you have any idea how you might go about helping me?"

"Honestly, no clue."

"I thought so. It's easier if you just stay out of the way."

Amane couldn't really argue with Mahiru's harsh assessment, so he tried to sit quietly on the sofa, but he found it impossible to settle down and do nothing.

It wasn't that Amane hadn't done anything at all—he'd finished cleaning his apartment the day before, and earlier he'd gone on a big shopping run, picking up ingredients for the *osechi* dishes along with enough food so that they wouldn't have to go out for a while. He had taken care of the more physical tasks, but at the moment, Mahiru was busy, and he wasn't doing much.

"You must be tired from moving all the furniture and appliances yesterday to clean, so please, just take it easy," Mahiru said without turning around, though Amane thought he heard a note of concern in her voice.

It appeared that Mahiru had already finished her own New Year's cleaning. Apparently, it hadn't taken much work at all since she always kept her place so tidy.

So that's the difference between someone who makes a habit of keeping things clean and someone who doesn't, Amane mused. *Guess I should've realized that earlier...*

"Well, even so, I feel bad about it."

"I really like cooking, so it's no trouble."

"Still..."

"It's fine; I'm having fun."

Amane was at a loss for how to react to Mahiru, who brushed him off, fully absorbed in her work.

"Mahiru, I went ahead and bought lunch."

It would have been unfair to expect Mahiru to prepare lunch when she had her hands full with the *osechi*, so Amane had gone to the convenience store. He'd figured there would be no problem with a simple meal of sandwiches, since Mahiru didn't eat that much anyway.

Mahiru had already taken off her apron. She must have been planning to take a break, so the timing seemed just about perfect.

"Thanks for going to the trouble," Mahiru said as she stepped into the living room. Her break would double as lunchtime. "I'm really sorry for not getting around to making lunch."

"Come on, I'm definitely the one who should be apologizing, with you making all that *osechi*. Here, let's eat. How's a sandwich and café au lait sound?"

"That's fine, thank you," Mahiru said as she accepted the food, then took a seat beside him on the couch.

"So about how much have you gotten done so far?" Amane asked.

"Well, I'm using a lot of premade ingredients, and I'm trying not to limit the number of dishes, so...I'd say I'm nearly finished. After this, there are a lot of things that need to rest or chill in the fridge. You seem to like sweet rolled omelets, Amane, so I made those by hand."

"How did you know?"

"You like all the other egg dishes I make. I didn't think that rolled omelets would be the exception."

He surmised that she had cooked them specially in the oven. He had heard it humming earlier and wondered what she was making.

"You like the ones that are slightly sweet, right?"

"You know me too well."

"It's not surprising that I would learn your tastes after several months," Mahiru said as she bit into her ham and lettuce sandwich. It made him very happy to hear that.

As Amane started eating the rice ball he had bought for himself, he looked over into the kitchen. His eyes landed on the smallish multi-tiered food boxes that Mahiru had brought over with her.

She must be planning to pack the food into those boxes.

He hadn't expected her to go so far as to bring out the special boxes for all the food—after all, she lived alone, just like him—so he had been a little shocked to see the fancy-looking containers all painted with lacquer and decorated with gold leaf.

"Seriously, I can't thank you enough. How do I put this…? This past year, I've gotten to enjoy food in a way I never could have imagined when I first started living alone."

"And here I thought you were doing just fine on your own."

"Rude. You know better than anyone how I was surviving off convenience store meals."

"It certainly wasn't healthy. That's for sure." Mahiru let out an exasperated sigh, but she also wore a knowing smile, which caught Amane by surprise. "Well, now that I'm here," she added, "I won't let you fall back into your old unhealthy habits, all right?"

"Who are you, my mom?"

"It's your own fault for living like that. Next year you're really going to learn how to eat properly. Do I make myself clear?" Mahiru's eyes shone with sudden enthusiasm.

Amane realized that she had just announced her intention to spend the coming year with him as well. The thought made him feel terribly self-conscious, and he found himself looking away.

However, Mahiru must have interpreted that gesture as a

reluctance to give up his slothful ways because she promptly scowled at Amane, who found himself struggling to awkwardly explain himself.

Mahiru finished making and packing up all the *osechi* dishes by around sunset and then set about preparing the New Year's noodles, which just entailed boiling the noodles and readying the toppings, since they had bought precut raw noodles.

She had some *kamaboko* fish cake left over from the *osechi*, so that was a perfect addition. All there was left to do was parboil the spinach and slice the green onion.

The most labor-intensive part was the shrimp tempura, but Mahiru seemed to be having no trouble as she fried them all up.

"I also had some *kabocha* left over, so I'm going to fry that while I'm at it."

"Man…these are gonna be some serious New Year's noodles."

"Sometimes it's fun to make stuff like this," Mahiru said as she finished serving up the noodles. They looked far more splendid than anything most people would normally eat at home.

She had made two large pieces of shrimp tempura per bowl, and the bonus *kabocha* tempura was crisped to perfection. There was plenty of spinach and green onion, and the *kamaboko* fish cake was cut into a decorative fan shape.

Amane noticed that Mahiru liked to keep her tempura crispy, as both of their portions had been placed on separate plates rather than directly in the bowl with the noodles. He was grateful for this small, thoughtful act.

"Wow!"

"Please, eat up."

Perhaps concerned that the noodles wouldn't be enough to satisfy

Amane's appetite, Mahiru had also served all the leftover bits from the *osechi* dishes on a small plate.

Amane watched Mahiru take her seat, then they both pressed their hands together to give thanks for the food before digging into their noodles.

Even though Mahiru had said that the soba had come premade, she must have picked out high-quality noodles. Amane could smell the rich fragrance of buckwheat with every bite. The broth wasn't too thick or too thin, and it was seasoned so well he sighed with delight. It warmed him from the depths of his belly. The perfect dish for a cold day.

"Ah...now this is what the end of the year should feel like..."

He took a sip of broth and sighed...mumbling quietly to himself.

He was certainly enjoying the chance to sit back and watch TV while eating his noodles, awaiting the arrival of the New Year.

It was also his family's custom every year to eat New Year's noodles and spend New Year's Eve watching the year-end musical specials on television, so Amane was glad that he could keep the tradition going.

But tonight he was not sitting with his family—instead, there was a beautiful girl beside him.

"When you eat New Year's noodles, it hits you all at once that the year's really ending, doesn't it?" Mahiru asked.

"I know what you mean...," Amane replied. "So much happened this year."

Of course, he was mostly talking about his burgeoning relationship with Mahiru.

When he'd first started living alone, he couldn't possibly have imagined such a beautiful girl fixing him such delicious meals.

"Oh, because this was the year you started living alone, right, Amane? That must have been difficult."

"You, on the other hand, never seem to have any trouble, do you?"

"Well, that's because I can more or less do everything for myself. It's a disaster for someone like you, trying to live on your own even though you don't know how to do anything."

"Uh...that's true, but..."

"You really are the definition of hopeless, aren't you?"

The expression on Mahiru's face was gentle as she scolded him, more charming than exasperated. She didn't seem burdened by taking care of Amane. She just looked...content.

"...I owe you for everything you've done this year."

He repeated the words of thanks that he had said to her on Christmas, and Mahiru smiled slightly.

"And don't you ever forget it."

Her quick and unconditional agreement prickled slightly in his chest, but his saving grace was that Mahiru clearly didn't mean anything.

"...I hope you'll help me out next year, too."

"I know I'll need to. If I wasn't around, you'd barrel headlong into an unhealthy and slovenly lifestyle again in no time."

"I can't deny that."

"...If you're aware of it, then you ought to do better..."

"I'll aspire to do so in the coming year."

Even if he did put his mind to it, Amane had a feeling that Mahiru's constant caretaking would quickly erode any desire to fend for himself. Of course, he couldn't say that out loud, so he pushed the thought to the back of his mind.

He'd do his best to keep his place tidy, but there was no doubt that he would still be depending on her for meals. He had become entirely domesticated, and the fact that he was painfully aware of this development didn't make it any less true. Plus, Mahiru always laughed at him whenever he said he was going to try to improve himself.

Amane made a sour face, but Mahiru just smiled slightly, as if she was savoring the moment.

"The New Year's almost upon us."

"Looks like it."

They had finished eating their New Year's noodles and sat on the sofa watching the annual end-of-the-year musical showcase on television. Before either of them realized it, the new day—and the New Year—was just moments away.

Time had passed much faster than Amane had expected while he was occupied watching Mahiru quietly enjoy the show. Apparently, she wasn't very familiar with current pop music, possibly because she didn't watch much TV in general.

The screen switched over to a scene of a temple bell—a clear sign the year was about to end. The great bell began ringing. Seated next to him, Mahiru quietly listened to the chimes, eyes lowered.

As the bell rang the one hundred and seventh time—

The instant that the new day began, Mahiru turned to him, sat up properly, and bowed. "Happy New Year," she said.

Caught up in the moment, Amane also straightened up and gave her the same formal New Year's greeting. "Happy New Year... It feels kind of strange, huh? Spending it together."

"Heh-heh, I suppose it does," Mahiru replied. "I hope you'll look after me this year as well."

"Of course... Though, it feels like I should really be the one asking you that, eh?"

"I can't argue with that."

Mahiru let out a giggle, and Amane shot her a slightly awkward grin. Then the smartphone he had on his lap began to vibrate. His messaging app had several notifications—New Year's greetings had come in from Itsuki and Chitose.

Mahiru's phone also vibrated. She had only just met his friends and hadn't exchanged contact info with Chitose yet, so she must have been getting messages from a friend Amane didn't know.

In recent years, the convenience of sending New Year's greetings via phone message had become really popular.

"I'm just going to reply to this."

"Same."

Amane figured that Mahiru had probably received a lot of messages. Yet somehow he also had the feeling that she wasn't in the habit of giving boys her contact information.

Amane watched Mahiru's practiced fingers flit deftly across her phone as she typed out her responses. "It's times like these that you finally seem like a regular high school girl," he remarked before checking his own phone.

The messages from Itsuki and Chitose were the bog-standard 'Happy New Year' followed by needless prying. "Did you spend the New Year holiday getting friendly with Lady Shiina?" As usual, Itsuki was disconcertingly perceptive.

Amane sent a reply denying it.

Immediately, he got a mocking response from Itsuki, accusing him of lying. For a while, the two friends carried on a lively text conversation. Itsuki would make certain allegations that Amane would deny every time, and then…he felt a weight flop down against his upper arm.

A sweet fragrance wafted over him.

The sudden contact startled him. He glanced timidly to the side, not believing it could be true…only to confirm that Mahiru was indeed leaning against him, fast asleep.

—Wait, wait, wait!

Amane didn't say anything out loud, but he was already beginning to panic on the inside.

Mahiru had dozed off at his place before, but who could have ever imagined that she would do so here and now, right beside him, pressed up against his shoulder?

It was obvious what had happened.

They had stayed up quite late, past twelve thirty AM. Mahiru, who observed a strict routine, probably wasn't used to being awake at this hour. Moreover, she had spent most of the day bustling about making the *osechi* dishes and must have been exhausted, even if she didn't show it on the surface. She simply hadn't had the strength to fight off the sandman any longer.

Amane completely understood—but to fall asleep now of all times!

Dozing against Amane's shoulder, Mahiru wore a truly peaceful expression, completely oblivious to his confusion and consternation. Her long eyelashes and cute nose and pink lips all had a soft vulnerability to them that Amane hadn't noticed before.

It wasn't the first time he'd seen her sleeping face, but he had never observed her from such close range, and the sight froze him in place.

"Mahiru...," he said hesitantly. "Mahiru, wake up."

There was no response.

Mahiru must have been incredibly tired. It seemed that her fatigue had dragged her down into the deepest oceans of slumber. He called out to her and nudged her with his shoulder, but the girl showed no sign of waking.

Even when he tapped her shoulder and gently shook her body, Mahiru didn't stir.

His attempts to rouse her caused her to start pitching forward after slipping off his arm. In a panic, Amane caught her and pulled her back toward him...which was fine, but now he found himself embracing her. His alarm only grew.

…Wow, she smells amazing…

After dinner, Mahiru had briefly gone back to her place to freshen up, and the floral fragrance of her shampoo that mingled with her natural scent was making Amane tremendously uncomfortable. And he couldn't help but notice how soft she was, pressed up against him.

Amane was not handling this well.

He had tried to wake her, but she had fallen too deeply asleep, and he was reluctant to try to rouse her more forcefully.

What should I do?

The New Year had barely started, and Amane was already facing an unbelievable dilemma.

He looked down at the girl sleeping in his arms with grim determination. She was still out cold. *She must really trust me to drift off like that without a care,* Amane realized. It was enough to make him want to bang his head against the wall in frustration and embarrassment as his sense of reason began to fail him.

No matter how he tried, his attention kept straying back to the distinct feeling of her slender body pressed against his. It was firm, but with a feminine softness to it, and had a particularly intoxicating voluptuousness where their chests met…

—What the heck should I do?

Not only was Amane utterly unprepared for his present situation, the unimaginable softness brushing against him was quickly wearing away at any remaining composure he thought he possessed.

This was the first time he had ever realized how soft and supple and nice-smelling girls could be…and even thinking about how he felt was enough to send his mind spinning into chaos. It was like one big feedback loop.

Even so, he still felt compelled to do something. He had a feeling that there was not going to be an easy way out of this one, so Amane tried to clear his mind and steel his resolve.

At the moment, there were three ways he could think of to approach this.

1. Wake Mahiru forcefully.
2. Carry Mahiru home.
3. Let Mahiru sleep in his own bed—and spend the night on the couch himself.

The first option gave him pause. He didn't like the idea of jostling Mahiru awake when she was obviously so very tired. What's more, he was the one responsible for wearing her out, so if it was possible, he wanted to let her rest.

At first glance, option two initially seemed like it would be the least awkward, but he was really uncomfortable with the idea of searching through Mahiru's pockets for the key to her apartment and entering a girl's home without permission. He also suspected that Mahiru would not be too pleased to discover that he'd decided that on his own.

Option three, letting her stay over, was seemed like a safer choice that would be easy to pull off, but…he was not at all emotionally prepared to have a beautiful girl sleeping in his bed. It didn't matter how they normally got along. Amane felt like the innocent charm of her sleeping face was driving him mad.

The thought of such a stunning beauty asleep on his pillow was almost unbearable for this growing boy. Some of the images that crossed his mind were guilt-inducing.

Still, there was no denying it was the most promising option and the most considerate compromise that Amane could think of.

He steadied himself for the task, then gently wrapped his hands around Mahiru's back and under her knees and slowly lifted her.

She was sleeping soundly and was as light as a feather. Of course he would never say so out loud, but Mahiru felt almost ephemeral in his arms.

He had learned firsthand that she probably wouldn't wake up too easily, but just in case, Amane tried to keep her as steady as possible while he gingerly carried her to his room. It took both hands to cradle her, so opening the door proved quite the challenge, but eventually Amane successfully laid Mahiru on his bed.

Her delicate body sunk into the mattress.

Once Amane had covered her with a blanket and comforter, she was all set up for the night. He didn't see any indication she was going to wake up, and all he could hear was her regular, rhythmic breathing. Her face was beautiful as always, but seeing it so cherubic in sleep was making Amane's heart jump in his chest.

He courteously tucked her in, then crouched down beside the bed.

...*It's too much.*

Having a girl sleeping in his bed, remembering the soft feeling of her body against his, seeing her adorable and defenseless sleeping face, then realizing just how much she must trust him to fall asleep in his apartment—that and a million other things were running through his mind.

Of course, he was grateful she believed in him, but at the same time, he couldn't help but think that she only saw him as a safe and hopeless nuisance, a harmless little boy.

Amane glanced over at her and noted the tranquil expression on her sleeping face. She was utterly oblivious to his inner turmoil.

She has no idea how I feel.

And she's let down her guard too much.

...*I could climb into that bed right now if I wanted to...*

The thought lasted only a moment before he pushed it out of his mind. Of course it would be wrong, on so many levels. And he knew that the moment Mahiru woke up and discovered them sleeping together, she would never talk to him ever again. He shuddered at the thought of her soft eyes turning cold and scornful.

That is definitely a bad idea.

But maybe, instead of that, if…just a little……would be okay, wouldn't it?

He extended a hand toward Mahiru's head.

Smooth, sleek, glossy—those were the words that came to mind as he slid his fingers over her long, soft, vibrant hair without hitting a single snag.

She must work hard to keep it like this, huh…?

Feeling both admiration and a shudder of fear at the enormous efforts demanded by femininity, Amane let his fingertips glide slowly across Mahiru's cheek. Her porcelain skin was surprisingly cool, at least compared to Amane's fingers. When the brief caress was over, Amane looked down and saw that a slight smile had graced Mahiru's tranquil face.

"Good night."

I'm sure she'll be surprised when she wakes up in the morning tomorrow…or actually today, I guess. Considering what he had just gone through, he figured that she could live with a little surprise.

I really am hopeless…

Amane flashed a troubled smile, then gently reached out to stroke Mahiru's soft cheek one more time.

Chapter 2

The Defenseless Angel and the Start of the New Year

When Amane awoke in the morning, all was quiet.

He could hear the cries of birds outside, but there was no sign from his bedroom that Mahiru was up yet.

It was already past dawn, but maybe because she was exhausted from the night before, Mahiru seemed to still be sleeping soundly.

Amane had only managed to get some brief shut-eye—the persistent thought of Mahiru in his bed made true rest elusive—and he had ended up drifting off, lingering on the edge of sleep until deciding to get up.

The restless night wasn't particularly taxing on him physically, so that was fine, but the whole situation was trying in another way. This was the first time he had ever let a girl stay over at his place, never mind having one sleep in his bed. Naturally, he was incredibly anxious.

…I mean, what am I even supposed to do in a situation like this?

He was pretty sure that Mahiru had only allowed herself to fall asleep because she considered him a safe and harmless guy, but Amane was a guy nonetheless, a fact that he wished she would acknowledge more often.

He really regretted not waking her and sending her back home, but it was no use now.

Amane sighed and stretched to work out the knots in his body after spending the night on the sofa, then stood up slowly.

For the time being, he thought he would look in on Mahiru. Well, his main goal was actually to grab a change of clothes, but he decided to check on her while he was in there.

Ever so slowly, he opened the bedroom door.

Inside, it was quiet. Mahiru was just as he had left her, still sleeping in his bed.

If there had been any change, it was that she must have turned over several times in her sleep, because now she was lying on her side, and her hair was spread across the sheets like a flowing river of gold.

Amane knelt down to look at Mahiru more closely. Her sleeping breaths were even and serene.

She looks so innocent when she's asleep.

Mahiru often wore a calm expression, perhaps because she usually had her guard up, but...her sleeping face was the picture of tranquility. Again, he felt the urge to reach out and pet her.

...She really is cute like this...

Of course, she was undeniably beautiful any time of day, but seeing her in such a vulnerable state plucked at Amane's heartstrings in a very different way.

He wanted to stroke her smooth hair and poke at her soft cheeks.

She was usually so proper and reserved, with no gaps or cracks in her facade, so catching her in a defenseless state like this made him want to mess with her a little.

Without putting any thought into the matter, Amane stretched a hand out toward her and pressed the tip of his finger against her cheek, which looked so soft. Mahiru's skin was as silky as it had been the night before. He almost wanted to go on touching her forever. In the back of his mind, he knew he needed to be delicate, but the softness of her skin was spellbinding and made him want to dote on her…

Mahiru, who had been sleeping quietly, suddenly let out a hoarse but endearing groan and looked at Amane with bleary, caramel-colored eyes…or at least, she seemed to look in Amane's direction. He thought that her cherubic face appeared even more innocent in repose. She stared absently for a moment, eyes blank and cloudy with sleep, and then frowned and settled back down.

When Amane started to pull his hand away, Mahiru stirred, and her cheek brushed against his fingers again. "…Nn…" A dainty sigh rose in her throat.

To Amane, it almost seemed like she was saying *Don't go.*

Of course, Mahiru was obviously still half asleep. She would definitely never act like this under any normal circumstances.

Even so, Amane thought that her movements reminded him of an affectionate kitten. The day had only just begun, and already his brain was failing him. He couldn't decide whether to pull back or keep caressing her cheek. Despite all sense and reason, his heart was really leaning toward the latter. After all, he rarely got to see Mahiru this unguarded, and he wanted to see how much he could get away with.

But Amane knew that if Mahiru caught him acting on his desire, she wouldn't listen to a word he had to say. He knew without a doubt that this would all make her incredibly uncomfortable, so he stopped short.

Mahiru seemed to be coming around slowly, but she was obviously not awake just yet. She hadn't moved, and her cheek was still pressed against Amane's fingers.

©Hanekoto

He had come into the room looking to check on her and maybe grab a change of clothes while he was at it. How had he ended up doing something like this? Amane felt his cheeks grow hot as it fully dawned on him just how unspeakably creepy he was acting.

"Nn-ngh…"

After another moment, Mahiru's eyelids finally started to flutter open again…

"…Ah."

They locked eyes.

Mahiru's gaze flicked from Amane, who was leaning over her, to his extended finger. She immediately sat bolt upright.

"M-morning," Amane stammered.

"…G-good morning…"

"You fell asleep at my place, so I let you stay the night here, but I didn't have any ulterior motives and I swear I didn't do anything, so really, I hope you can appreciate all that…" Amane said, the words pouring out in a rush as he struggled to explain.

As she listened to Amane's jumbled account, Mahiru stayed quiet, but her cheeks quickly flushed bright red as it dawned on her where she had slept, and she tugged at a corner of the futon, practically hiding herself with it.

Finding even that small gesture charming, Amane quickly turned away.

What is happening *here?*

Even though he had lent her a bed for the night, he was starting to feel bad. He knew that he had been wrong to touch her without permission. But it had only been for a moment, and he had absolutely no intention of taking it any further.

Amane looked back at Mahiru. His heart was pounding in his chest. He didn't know if it was because he was smitten with her or from feeling guilty. He saw that her cheeks were still tinged red, and she was staring at him with a sullen look...or not quite sullen. It seemed like she had something to say to him.

"...Amane, do you like touching my cheeks?"

"Huh?"

"I mean, you touched me at Christmas and then again yesterday when I fell asleep, didn't you?"

"...So you were awake the whole time?"

The other night, when he had stroked her cheek...he'd thought that she'd been fast asleep. That she would never know he'd touched her. But she did, because she'd actually been awake at the time.

"Well, you see, I briefly woke up just as I was being lowered into bed... Moreover, how could I do anything else in a situation like that?"

"Weren't you worried about me...doing something?" Amane asked.

"...I never thought you would do anything like *that*, but...in order to confirm my suspicions, I pretended to be asleep."

Apparently, falling asleep in front of him had been some kind of test to determine whether he was really worthy of her trust. Ultimately, it seemed like she was leaning toward yes rather than no, for which he was glad.

Amane hoped she wouldn't test that out again. He really wasn't sure he would do any better the next time he was faced with controlling himself when she was that same charming vulnerability, either.

"...Well, I'm glad you haven't decided I'm totally shady. Also please don't try any more tests. I am a man, after all."

"Uh, I kn-know that, but—"

"Or maybe you were expecting me to try something?"

"Of course not!" Mahiru firmly denied, pulling the comforter back up around her. She was practically shaking, and Amane thought he'd seen her start to blush, just a little. He wisely swallowed the urge to make a joke about her being in his bed.

For now, it was probably a good idea to give Mahiru some space until she regained her composure.

After that inexplicable bout of awkwardness, Mahiru returned to her apartment to freshen up before coming back again. But it was obvious that she was still embarrassed because she refused to make eye contact with Amane. Every time he tried to catch her gaze, she turned away. Even though she was sitting on the sofa right next to him, it was like she was miles away.

"…Please forgive me," Amane said, stomach twisting in knots.

Mahiru quickly glanced over at him, then sighed softly. Maybe she wasn't as upset anymore; she was wearing her usual serene expression. "I'm not angry. You don't have to apologize, Amane."

"Well, I think—"

"I suppose I'm mostly upset with myself for being so careless, that's all. I really wish you hadn't seen me like that."

"Like…what? I thought you looked really sweet…"

Mahiru's dreaming face had reminded him why people called her an angel, but more importantly, he had discovered that just after she woke up, in the moments between sleep and wakefulness, her usual cool and collected demeanor gave way to a youthful innocence that he found extremely charming.

If anything, Amane wanted to see her like that again.

But it was clear that Mahiru was not happy that he'd seen her with her guard down. Before Amane could argue any further, she bit her lip hard and suddenly whacked him with a pillow. It didn't hurt or anything—it was obvious that Mahiru wasn't really trying—but it caught Amane by surprise.

"What the heck?"

"...You know, I hate that about you, Amane."

"Hate what? At least tell me what I did wrong."

"What you said... That's not the sort of thing that you can just say to a girl so casually, you know?"

"Well it's not like I would say that sort of thing to anyone else..."

The only girls Amane knew were Mahiru and Chitose. And sure, Chitose was cute, but Amane found her more annoying than anything else, and there was no need for him to praise her to her face anyway. So who else would he even talk to like that?

Amane could see that Mahiru was feeling defensive. He watched her reactions carefully as he continued. "Besides, you must be used to people saying those kinds of things about you, right?" He shrugged. "Why should it bother you now?"

After all, he had told Mahiru many times that he thought she was cute. It didn't seem like the kind of thing that would suddenly become a sticking point. She knew how beautiful she was.

She can't be that *embarrassed just because of a little compliment.*

That's what Amane thought, but for some reason, Mahiru was still wearing a sour face.

"Seriously, what's the matter?"

"...It's nothing."

She landed one final attack by whacking him again with the cushion, then Mahiru turned away sharply and said "I'm going to go make mochi soup" before putting on her apron and heading for the kitchen.

Amane couldn't do anything but squeeze the cushion and stare at Mahiru's back as she abruptly stalked out of the room.

By the time they finished eating the mochi soup, Mahiru was back to her usual self. The start of the meal had been rather uncomfortable, but both the soup and the assorted *osechi* dishes were so delicious that Amane had quickly forgotten everything else, and before he realized it, Mahiru's spirits had recovered.

As they moved from the table back to sitting together on the sofa, Amane asked, "By the way, are you planning to go for a shrine visit to start off the New Year, Mahiru?"

"Shrine visit? I wasn't really planning to go… I don't like crowds, you know. People always stare at me."

"That's because you're…"

He had been about to say "…because you're so beautiful," but the mood had only just recovered after his earlier faux pas, so he swallowed the words and only said "Well, I guess there's not a ton you can do about that" instead.

"Are you going to go to one, Amane?"

"I always went with my parents when I was back home, but I was just wondering whether I should go. I was thinking that it might be best to pass, at least on New Year's Day."

"Agreed."

"Chitose and Itsuki are having a cozy time at her place, so they're not around, and kids these days don't make a big deal out of the first shrine visit of the year anyway, you know? I think we can put it off."

Compared to the old days…for young people, especially those in their teens and twenties, first-day-of-the-year shrine visits were getting less and less popular. Amane and Mahiru wouldn't be especially strange for skipping out.

It wasn't exactly that he didn't want to go, but he knew that there would be too many people to be able to move comfortably and that the experience would just end up being exhausting, so he was thinking it would probably be better to go after the crowds thinned out a bit.

"Besides," Amane continued, "I want to spend the first three days of the New Year relaxing. I don't really care about holiday bargains or anything, either."

"Actually, I am sort of interested in the special blind bags some stores have," Mahiru mentioned.

"Are you going to a shopping mall or somewhere?"

She shook her head. "...I'm not brave enough to charge into those crowds."

"Agreed."

Amane replied in the same way Mahiru had a moment ago and leaned back into the sofa.

There was definitely no need to go anywhere just because it was New Year's Day.

Amane was perfectly content taking it easy at home. He preferred to avoid stressful situations, after all. And since they'd be spending the holiday together, he certainly wouldn't want for food or conversation.

Thinking to himself what a luxurious New Year's holiday this was turning out to be, Amane stole a glance at Mahiru sitting beside him as a small smile crept onto his face.

Chapter 3

Visiting Parents and the First Shrine Visit of the Year

"Can we visit your apartment tomorrow, Amane?"

Amane's father, Shuuto, sent that message at ten o'clock in the evening on January 3—after dinner and after Mahiru had gone home.

"It's all right that you didn't come home for the holiday, but I do want to see you. Besides, I heard about her from your mother, but I think I'd better say hello to your neighbor myself."

His father probably wanted to meet the person taking such good care of his son. And since Amane's mother had already discovered his relationship with Mahiru, and was actually in regular contact with her, Amane didn't see much point in refusing.

He no longer had anything to hide, and he didn't want to turn his parents away after not visiting for the holidays. Plus, Amane figured that the presence of his father should help keep his mother in check and prevent her from making a big scene. If nothing else, Amane was counting on him to help him avoid a repeat of her last exhausting visit.

Besides, Amane had a feeling that even if he did refuse his parents, his mother would come over to see Mahiru anyway, so after setting up a time with his father (who had been courteous enough to ask in advance) Amane sent Mahiru a heads-up message.

"Um, well, is it all right for me to be there during your family time? Won't I be intruding?"

The next day, Mahiru came over to Amane's apartment early. She seemed nervous.

That was only to be expected, in a way. Mahiru had been taking care of him...though phrasing it that way sounded a bit misleading... In any case, Mahiru had been spending a lot of time with him, and now his parents wanted to meet her.

She was already used to talking with his mother, or at least being talked at by his mother, but Amane's father would be joining this time. It was no surprise that she was nervous.

"Well, now that Dad is coming to say hello, and since Mom has taken such a liking to you, I'd appreciate it if you were here. Really, I need you here."

"Y-you say that, but..."

"I'm sure you would rather avoid it, but it'd really mean a lot to me if you'd put up with it just for a little while."

It was somewhat surreal to be introducing her to his parents, but they'd requested, and now there was no way around it.

He felt bad for taking up Mahiru's time, but he knew that his father was the type of person who likely wouldn't rest until he'd met her, so he hoped she wouldn't mind it too much.

"...I wonder what Shihoko has told him about me."

"Relax. I made sure to tell my dad that you are someone who helps me out a lot. Even if he gets the wrong idea, I've already told him that my mother's crazy ideas about you are not at all true."

Amane's mother seemed to have already decided that Mahiru was his bride-to-be and her very own future daughter-in-law. Amane had made sure to firmly deny everything coming out of her mouth. His father had laughed and said, "Shihoko has always had the bad habit of letting her imagination run wild." So apparently, he understood the situation.

Mahiru seemed relieved to hear that, and Amane smiled wryly as they waited. "Sorry about this."

Then, with perfect timing, the intercom rang.

His parents had already gotten past the lobby with their duplicate key, so he expected that they had come directly to his door.

At the sound of the chime, Mahiru shuddered in surprise, so Amane shot her a small smile to put her at ease and headed for the door. He took the chain off and unfastened the lock.

When he opened the door, there stood his parents, just as he remembered them.

"It's been half a year, Amane."

"Long time no see, Dad."

Amane greeted Shuuto's amicable smile with a slightly relieved grin of his own.

With his gentle demeanor, Shuuto was the type of person who somehow calmed things down just by being around. Amane relaxed a little simply seeing him there.

"You didn't seem nearly as happy to see your mother...," Shihoko said.

"That's because my mother forced her way in without so much as a warning. If you'd ever give me any notice, I would react normally."

The last time Shihoko had shown up, Mahiru had been at his place, and he'd tried to turn her away. If he'd been alone, he probably would have treated her a little nicer.

"Well anyway, come on in," Amane added. "What's with the package?"

"Oh, we brought you all sorts of things. But we can look at that later. Where's Mahiru?"

"Inside," Amane answered succinctly. After his parents had removed their shoes, he led them into the living room.

Mahiru seemed anxious as she looked over at them and blinked, wide-eyed, in understandable surprise.

Amane's father looked remarkably young. He didn't seem to be much past thirty, especially if you forgot that he had a teenage son, and had a youthful, handsome face. More than once, Amane had wished that he took more after his father, whose tender features made him seem like a well-mannered young man (though in actuality, he was middle-aged). When the two of them walked side by side, they looked more like distant brothers than father and son.

"Mahiru dear, it's been too long," Shihoko said.

"'Too long'? It's only been a month!" Amane remarked.

"I think that counts." Shihoko approached Mahiru wearing a beaming smile.

Mahiru stood straighter and greeted her with a formal "How good to see you again," wearing the faint smile that was an integral part of her public persona.

But her bewildered eyes were still straying toward Amane's father, standing next to Shihoko. Shuuto smiled warmly when he noticed Mahiru looking.

"Nice to meet you. I'm Amane's father, Shuuto Fujimiya. I've heard about you from Shihoko, Miss Shiina. Thank you for taking such good care of our son."

"Nice to meet you. I'm Mahiru Shiina. And I appreciate everything Amane does for me as well."

Shuuto bowed politely, and Mahiru introduced herself courteously.

Mahiru had probably been worried that Amane's father would be a lot like his mother, but Shuuto was a mild-mannered man with a good head on his shoulders, and he was doing his best to put Mahiru at ease.

Shuuto was generally the one who reined in Shihoko's wilder tendencies. Really, he was the only person she would listen to, which proved just how much she loved him.

"Goodness, you don't have to be so modest!" Shihoko interrupted. "Amane is a slob, after all."

"Geez, sorry I don't meet your standards...," Amane muttered.

"Come now, Shihoko, don't say things like that," his father said. "...And, Amane, this girl is taking care of you day in, day out, so I'm sure you're showing her the appropriate gratitude and appreciation, right?"

"As best I can."

"That's what I like to hear."

Shuuto, who had raised Amane to treasure women, had apparently been worried over whether his son was being considerate enough. Of course Amane would have found it unbearable to kick back while Mahiru did everything, so he did whatever he could for her.

Shuuto seemed reassured by Amane's answer and turned his gaze toward Mahiru again.

"...Truly, I must offer you my thanks. I hear you've been fixing my son's meals every day, and you were even kind enough to make *osechi* dishes for the holiday..."

"I'm always thanking her for that. I've been trying to show my appreciation every chance I get, too."

"It's true..." Mahiru nodded. "Amane's surprisingly considerate."

"Surprisingly?" Amane asked. "And what's so surprising about it?"

"Th-that is, I—I mean...," Mahiru stammered. "You seemed...a bit neglectful at first glance, but it turns out you actually pay rather close attention."

Amane found himself at a loss for words, unable to refute anything she said.

"The most important thing is that the two of you are getting along well," Shuuto said with a gentle smile. "Amane, make sure you're not being too much of a bother to Miss Shiina."

"...I know that."

"And, Miss Shiina, I'd like you to speak up right away if Amane gives you any trouble. My son might not seem like it, but he's really quite an earnest young man, so I believe he'll do his best to smooth over any...rough patches."

"Amane is a nice guy. I can't think of anything rough about him...well, maybe just a tiny bit..."

"He's not exactly the smoothest, eh?"

"No...he's not really disagreeable...more like, he's just a little hopeless."

Mahiru was fidgeting as if she was having a hard time saying what was on her mind. It made Amane want to cross-examine her.

What exactly is so hopeless that you had to say it like that?

For some reason that Amane didn't understand, Shihoko seemed to grasp what Mahiru getting at. She looked over at him with a broad grin. "Ah-haah!"

Amane couldn't do much more than glare at his mother in irritation.

"Here you are."

Amane's parents were guests in his apartment, so it was only natural to treat them as such. However, Mahiru had insisted on being the one to set out the tea, so Amane had left it in her capable hands.

Mahiru had brought her tea set over to his apartment so she could use it whenever she visited. Amane had never imagined it would be used for this, though.

Both of his parents were wearing warm smiles, seated on the sofa where Amane and Mahiru usually sat together.

"My goodness, thank you, Mahiru dear. You're quite skilled at hosting visitors, aren't you?"

"Y-yes."

"Though, really, that should be Amane's job, you know?"

Mahiru was doing it because when Amane tried brewing tea, it usually turned out much too bitter.

Still, Shihoko looked somewhat aghast.

"No, I wanted to do it, but…"

"Well, I suppose that's fine, since Amane never gets the water temperature right."

His mother was absolutely correct, but it made him a little irritated that she pointed it out so blatantly.

However, he couldn't deny the truth, so he stoically kept his mouth shut as Shihoko turned to him and smiled.

"Come to think of it, Amane, you've finally started calling sweetie Mahiru by her first name, haven't you?"

At this sudden observation, both Amane and Mahiru froze.

They had grown so comfortable talking to each other that they hadn't noticed, but last time they had seen Amane's mother, the two of them had still been addressing each other quite formally.

"…What's it matter?"

"I think it's great!" His mother beamed. "It's nice that you're getting more intimate." Without pressing the issue any further, Shihoko just sat and beamed at them.

Amane could feel his cheek begin to twitch. He almost wished she would just make fun of him. It would have been easier than dealing with his mother's wild assumptions and fabricated narratives.

"Shihoko dear, don't tease Amane so much," Amane's father interjected. "It's a bad habit of yours," he added.

"All right, honey. You know I just can't help myself." Amane's mother capitulated to his father without much resistance, a fact for which their long-suffering son was acutely grateful. "But it's wonderful, isn't it? To see our son getting on so well with a cute girl?"

"I'm more concerned about whether you might get carried away again, Shihoko darling."

"When that happens, you'll step in for me, won't you, Shuuto darling?"

"On some level, I wish you'd work on it if you're already aware it's an issue...but that's also part of what makes you the woman I fell in love with, so I suppose there's no helping it."

"Ho-ho...what a sly fox you are."

Even though he was glad Shihoko had eased up on him, Amane couldn't help but sigh as his parents drifted off into their own little world.

His father was fundamentally a sensible man, but he had the unfortunate habit of doting on his treasured wife, which sometimes made it a little awkward for anyone else stuck in the same room.

Fortunately, they only did this in front of family and didn't act so embarrassingly in public. On the other hand, this was supposed to be Amane's apartment, and he wished they would show a little more restraint. He was glad that his parents still had a strong relationship after so many years together, but they could have been more considerate about their public displays of affection.

Whenever they got like this, Amane didn't like to force himself in between them, so he simply sat down in the chair he had brought over from the dining room and sighed deeply again in resignation.

Mahiru also took a seat in the chair he had set up next to his, and asked Amane quietly, "...Your parents get along very well, don't they?"

"Sure do. I mean, they're not like that outside, but that's definitely how they are at home."

"I see," Mahiru answered with a peculiar smile, then looked over at Shihoko and Shuuto.

She didn't seem uncomfortable at all—just the opposite, in fact. Mahiru looked like she was staring at something dazzling and priceless. Amane thought he saw a touch of envy in her gaze as she smiled so faintly that the word *fleeting* didn't do it justice. Without thinking, Amane extended a hand toward hers—

"Oh, Amane, what is it?"

He immediately withdrew his hand as the sound of Shihoko's voice pulled him back to his senses.

"Don't ask me. You and Dad went off into your own world. The two of us could barely stand to look at you."

"Oh, are you jealous?"

"Not a chance. I was just thinking that you should get a room. In the privacy of your own home, preferably."

His mother didn't seem to have noticed that he had been on the verge of grabbing Mahiru's hand. Mahiru also seemed not to have noticed and forced a smile at Amane's words.

He didn't understand why he had instinctually reached out toward her. For some reason…he had felt like he couldn't bear the thought of leaving Mahiru all alone.

She was already back to her usual self, so Amane felt slightly relieved and put on his usual surly expression so that no one would be any the wiser.

"So are you satisfied now, having seen your son's face?" Amane demanded.

"I'm more satisfied seeing sweet Mahiru than you, Amane…" His mother leered.

"Hey..."

"I'm only joking. We still haven't accomplished our real mission yet, you know."

"Your real what now...?"

Amane had assumed that they had come over to simply exchange New Year's greetings and meet Mahiru, but his mother seemed to have some other goal in mind.

"You and Mahiru haven't been on your first shrine visit of the year yet, right?"

"We were planning to go after the crowds die down."

"I knew it! And you haven't been yet, either, right, Mahiru? I asked in my message."

"Right." Mahiru nodded.

"I thought that would be the case, so we brought kimonos!"

Apparently, his mother wanted to go on a shrine visit with Mahiru.

Shihoko was wearing a wide grin as Amane finally realized the reason why she had brought such a large bag with her. He sighed again. He'd lost count of how many times today.

Shihoko loved cute things, and she loved playing dress-up, so she'd probably been waiting for a chance like this.

Amane also recalled that his mother had a large number of kimonos at home. Apparently, she had brought some with her.

"I've always dreamed of putting a kimono on a daughter and going on a shrine visit together... Oh, I'm sure this one will suit you, Mahiru."

"Mom, you just want a dress-up doll."

"That's not true! But I really do want to dress up Mahiru. Look, this one would suit her so well!" Shihoko was full of confidence, and her opinion was correct, insofar as there were hardly any clothes that wouldn't suit Mahiru.

Amane had seen her in everything from boyish outfits to fancy getups on top of her usual girly outfits that featured plenty of frills and lace. As far as he could remember, each and every style seemed to suit Mahiru just fine. Apparently, beautiful people didn't need to be choosy about what they wore. It was not hard to imagine that traditional Japanese clothes would really suit her as well.

Amane was an only child, so his mother was obviously not going to pass up this chance to dress up the daughter of her dreams.

"...Well, if Mahiru says it's all right, how about you dress her up and go?"

"Why are you talking like you're not coming, Amane?"

"I can't; it'll be trouble if I go out with Mahiru and people from school see us together."

If it was only his parents and Mahiru, they would just look like any other family going on a shrine visit, so it wouldn't rouse any suspicions, but if Amane joined them, and someone from their class spotted him at the shrine with Mahiru, well, he imagined that the start of the winter semester would turn into something out of a nightmare.

No shrine visit was worth that risk.

"So it'll be all right as long as no one finds out?"

"I suppose, but I'm pretty sure it'd be really... Uh, wait. I don't like where this is going, Mom..."

"Heh-heh! I came prepared for situations just like this!"

"What situations?!"

He had thought that she'd brought an awful lot of luggage for only kimonos and underclothes and accessories. Apparently, she had brought even more stuff so she could play dress-up with Amane as well.

"Your father is also very excited, you know."

"Dad..."

"We don't get to go out together very often," Amane's father said, "and it is our family's tradition, after all, so I'd like us to all go together."

When he put it that way, it was difficult to refuse.

Amane's father cared a great deal about family traditions. He would feel bad for refusing to go along after both his parents made it clear how much they wanted it.

"But look—"

"It's fine, dear. You just let your mother take care of it. I'll make you look like a stylish young man. I promise you won't even resemble the old Amane!"

"Isn't that basically the same as saying I'm not stylish now?"

"Of course, you've got good features because you take after your father, but your haircut and clothes are so unfashionable. I'd say you look gloomy."

"I didn't ask."

Amane was painfully aware of his drab appearance, but he looked like this because he liked to, so he didn't appreciate the criticism.

"You'd think that someone so handsome would have an easy time looking cool, but you're a troublesome case, Amane..."

"That's none of your business."

"It's such a waste...right, Mahiru dear? Wouldn't you like to see Amane all tidied up?"

"Huh?"

As the conversation suddenly shifted to her, Mahiru became visibly flustered.

Amane wished that his mother wouldn't prod at Mahiru so aggressively, but she continued needling the poor girl.

"Once Amane is all dressed up, I think you'll see him in a whole new light, too, Mahiru. He may not look it, but Amane's got a fairly handsome face, you know? Personality-wise, he's got some work to do, but he does resemble Shuuto, and he knows how to be a gentleman, so if you train him well, I think he could turn out quite nice."

"Ah, um…I…suppose so…?" Mahiru stammered.

"And don't you want to go on the first shrine visit of the year together?"

"W-well I…um…I do want to go, but…"

"Hey, how could you double-cross me like that?" Amane whined.

He'd been counting on her to consider what might happen in the worst-case scenario and reject his parents' proposal.

Mahiru glanced at the beleaguered Amane. "…If Amane doesn't want to, it's fine," she said in a quiet, slightly discouraged voice, frowning.

Amane choked. She was trying to hide it, but he could tell that Mahiru was disappointed. It wasn't anything dramatic; just a subtle change in her expression. Looking at her long eyelashes fluttering over her downcast eyes, Amane felt a powerful knot of guilt tighten in his chest.

His mother shot him a look of condemnation, as if to say *You made sweet Mahiru sad!* and his father wore an expression that said *It would be easier to fold here.*

Amane groaned quietly and simply said, "…All right."

When Mahiru made a face like that, there was nothing to do but give in.

"Okay, you're all set."

Shihoko had been tinkering wildly with Amane's hair and clothes, until he was quite exhausted by the time he was finally set free.

It had been pure agony for him, who wasn't much interested in clothes, but when he checked himself in the mirror, he could see that his suffering had been worth it. Staring back at him was a handsome young man, completely unlike the usual Amane.

The outfit Shihoko had chosen for him was a dark-gray Chesterfield coat over a white turtleneck, paired with black slacks—clean and casual.

Since this was supposed to be an auspicious New Year's event, she had apparently thought it was critical that he dress up a little. Amane usually didn't like especially colorful clothing, so this subdued, monochrome arrangement pleased him.

He checked his hairstyle, too, and saw that his mother's skill with a flat iron and some styling wax had really worked wonders with his long bangs. His eyes had emerged from their usual hiding spot behind his hair, and the impression he gave off was much brighter now that you could actually see his whole face. The extra volume in his hair plus the excellent styling made him look more dignified and refined as well.

The person in the mirror wasn't the Amane who got teased by his mother and Itsuki for being gloomy, but a bright young man who Amane had never seen before.

"You can turn into such a good-looking young man with just a little work, so I wonder why you don't do it?"

"Because I don't want to."

"You can really be such a grouch sometimes. Your face is usually dour, so unless you smile, you won't look good, you know?"

Being called dour stung, but Amane couldn't argue with the facts.

"All right, I'm going to go put the finishing touches on Mahiru, so you go wait in the living room."

Amane had been busy in his room, so he didn't have any idea how Mahiru was getting on. She had gone back to her apartment to dress herself, presumably to quite a high standard.

He watched his mother leave the room, then looked himself over in the mirror again.

He hadn't gotten dressed up like this in a long time, so he didn't resemble himself.

"...Well, I guess it's not bad."

He was sure he'd still look shabby standing next to Mahiru, but this was a big improvement.

Playing with his bangs a little, now that they weren't hanging in front of his eyes, Amane muttered under his breath that sprucing himself up like this from time to time probably wouldn't be a bad thing.

After waiting in the living room with his father for the better part of an hour, Amane heard the front door open.

He had heard that women's preparations could take quite a lot of time and effort, so he hadn't been particularly unhappy with the wait itself, but he was still a bit worried about leaving Mahiru alone and whether his mother might have crossed any lines.

Finally, thought Amane as he stood up from the sofa and looked toward the entryway, just as Mahiru quietly arrived in the living room.

The moment he laid eyes on her, he was stunned.

Mahiru didn't normally wear traditional Japanese clothing, so he had never had the chance to see her in it.

He had thought for sure that a kimono would look good on her, but—he hadn't expected this.

According to his mother, it would be difficult to move through a crowd in a long-sleeved kimono, so she had chosen something shorter. With its light-pink color and small, repeating pattern of plum blossoms, the kimono suited Mahiru so well that it was hard to believe it didn't actually belong to her.

Mahiru didn't normally wear much pink, but it gave her an air of refinement and femininity.

Her light-colored hair had been left out in long bangs on the sides, and the rest had been gathered into a bun and decorated with a *kanzashi* hair clip. Swaying across the pure-white nape of her neck, the accessory accentuated the girlishness of the ensemble and gave her a distinctly feminine allure.

The elegant outfit, coupled with makeup that had been judiciously applied to enhance her natural good looks, elevated Mahiru to the pinnacle of grace and beauty.

"So?" Amane's mother beamed. "I think we made her look very cute. Sweet Mahiru is so lovely to begin with, and dolling her up really had quite the effect."

"Yes, it certainly suits her, dear," his father quickly agreed.

Mahiru had her eyes cast downward, looking rather embarrassed by all the praise. Even that movement had something alluring about it.

Beauty can really be terrifying.

"Come on, Amane, say something."

"I think it looks good."

There was obviously no way he could possibly say what he really thought, especially not right there in front of his parents, so Amane kept his praise safely subdued.

His mother looked extremely dissatisfied.

"...That won't do at all!" she insisted.

"Oh, be quiet." Amane turned away. He was not going to engage with his mother any further.

Shihoko gave an exasperated sigh at her son's behavior, but perhaps because she knew him quite well, she seemed to agree to let it go.

"Good grief. Anyway, Mahiru darling, what do you think? Amane looks like a whole new person, right?"

"Y-yes. This is completely different..."

"And to think even though he would be so popular if he put in the effort to look like this all the time, he doesn't ever bother. Really, he's only harming himself."

Amane thought this was none of her business, but his mother sighed heavily again, as if she truly regretted the loss of potential.

"I'm so disappointed in Amane—he has the good fortune to take after his father, and yet he doesn't even try to put it to good use. What a waste!"

"Come now, Shihoko," his father said gently. "Amane's growing up in his own way."

"If he's growing up, then shouldn't he want to be popular?"

"If I had to guess, I'd say Amane is the type who is perfectly fine spending time with just one other person rather than bothering with a crowd."

"I guess."

Amane's father had tried to stall Shihoko, but that only fueled her wildest delusions.

It was true Amane preferred to hang out one-on-one rather than tag along in a big group... Apparently, that was something he had gotten from his father, and he really did think it was best, but if he said as much, especially now, it would sound like he was saying the person he preferred most was Mahiru...

His mother's radiant smile turned into a grimace, and she turned away.

Amane wondered why he had to put up with her unfair cynicism, but as a practical matter, he was well aware that other people looked at him the same way.

At the very least, Amane could say that Mahiru was a special case. That was the truth, but—

He snuck a glance at Mahiru, quickly, so she wouldn't notice, and sighed softly.

I guess I do like her, in a sense, he thought. *I mean, what's not to like about her?*

However, that was quite a different matter than declaring feelings of love.

"Mom, there is absolutely nothing going on, I'm telling you. So how about you stop it with the crazy accusations and go get the car ready."

"What an ungrateful child you are…really! Well, all right, I suppose. Shuuto, let's go prepare the car, shall we?"

"Sounds like a plan."

Amane had apparently succeeded in changing the subject, as both parents left to make ready for their departure.

He was leaving it up to his parents to decide which shrine they were going to, and he watched their backs as they left his apartment to head for the parking lot.

"…I've got the essentials in my bag, so I don't need much getting ready. How about you, Mahiru?"

"Everything I need is in this handbag, so I'm ready, too."

"Gotcha."

They were suddenly alone again, so with a slightly anxious feeling, Amane locked up the windows and unplugged nonessential appliances from the walls.

Once he had turned off the living room lights, he looked at Mahiru again.

As always, it was immediately apparent she was a beauty. He doubted whether there was another girl in the world who looked as good in a kimono.

He hadn't been comfortable praising her in front of his parents, but Amane was sure that anyone who saw her would agree that Mahiru was particularly beautiful in traditional Japanese dress.

"Is something the matter, Amane?"

"Oh, no, I was just thinking it really suits you. You look like an old-fashioned beauty from a painting or something. The outfit's cute, and I think you're really lovely."

He had learned from his father that when a girl was smartly dressed, compliments were in order, so he knew he should have praised her look the moment he saw her, but he had been too embarrassed to do it in front of his parents.

Once Amane had voiced his honest appraisal, Mahiru dramatically blinked several times, then blushed and pursed her lips tightly.

Recalling the last time she had reacted like that, Amane smiled bitterly.

"Ah, you don't like being complimented, right? Sorry."

"Th-that's not it, but... Amane, you're fairly—"

"Fairly what?"

"...It's nothing."

She abruptly turned away.

Amane wondered what was going on with her, but she didn't look like she was going to elaborate, so Amane quietly finished closing up the apartment and accompanied Mahiru to the door.

She seemed to have given some thought to the fact that they'd be walking around, because she was wearing boots instead of the traditional sandals. Her choice of footwear blended Japanese and western elements in her outfit, and she looked all the more adorable for it.

Mahiru somehow wiggled into her boots, as her hair accessory swung back and forth with a rustling sound, and Amane, who had gone out first to hold the door, found himself suddenly quite close to her.

Mahiru caught him by surprise when she stood up on her tiptoes and gingerly leaned even closer to him.

Thinking that maybe she wanted to tell him something, Amane

shut the door and locked it, then bent over to lend her his ear. Mahiru cupped her palms around her mouth and whispered into his ear.

"Amane—"

"Hmm?"

"Um... You look good, too, you know?"

That was all she said before slipping past him and briskly heading for the elevator. Amane promptly banged his head against his front door.

"...That's not fair."

Amane's heart was pounding like an alarm going off in his chest, his face was burning, and his forehead hurt. Mahiru had set him ablaze in a single breath. This was her revenge.

His parents looked at him suspiciously as he hustled to catch up to them in the parking lot.

When they arrived at a famous shrine located in an area a little less than an hour away, there weren't as many people as they had seen on television, but the crowds still seemed practically endless.

"Well, it's thinned out quite a bit, but I'd say there are still plenty here, eh?" Amane's mother remarked.

"There sure are...," Amane agreed.

"Mahiru darling, careful not to stray. We'll keep an eye on you, too, and we all have smartphones, so I think finding one another would be easy enough. But even so, I want us all to visit the shrine together, of course."

"Okay."

Dressed in a kimono, Mahiru had the hardest time moving out of all of them. The restrictive garment forced her to take small steps and walk slowly. At least she was wearing boots instead of sandals.

They didn't necessarily have to push their way through the crowd,

©Hanekoto

but it was tight enough that it was easy to run into people, so they had to proceed with caution.

"All right, shall we get going?"

Shihoko was leading the way through the crowd, and she headed first for the ablution pavilion where they would purify their hands and mouths with water. As expected, Mahiru was already attracting attention from many people.

More than a few people were dressed in kimonos, so Mahiru didn't stand out much for wearing one…but that wasn't the issue.

She drew people's eyes even in her school uniform, when she wasn't dressed up at all. Now that she looked like an aristocratic beauty in traditional Japanese clothing, she obviously garnered a lot of attention. Even her motions as she cleaned her mouth were graceful. Practically everyone in the shrine was staring.

"…Is something the matter?"

"No, nothing."

Though Amane was thinking it was all rather interesting, he didn't say as much, and he cleansed his hands and mouth just as his parents had, then followed after them as they walked on ahead.

He was doing his best to match pace with Mahiru, but as expected for someone who didn't ordinarily wear Japanese clothes, the long hem was giving her some difficulty, and the shrine was still quite crowded, so she was progressing much more slowly than usual.

"Mahiru, are you all right?"

"Yes, this is… Aaah!"

She was getting bumped around by the other shrine-goers, which kept knocking her off-balance and threatened to topple her outright, so Amane extended an arm to assist.

"You don't seem to be all right."

Of course she was uncomfortable walking around in a strange and complicated getup.

"…Sorry."

"Here, give me your hand."

Amane reached for one small hand that was peeking out of her kimono sleeve. Mahiru looked up at him, and he nearly pulled his hand back, but she quickly pressed her palm into his, keeping her eyes on him the whole time. He stared right back at her, though he was not entirely sure why.

Mahiru squeezed Amane's hand tightly and looked away.

He tilted his head questioningly, and they followed the flow of the crowd for a moment, until they were about to arrive in front of the offertory box, so Amane tucked whatever small doubts he had away in his heart and focused on the sensation of her hand in his.

"You were praying for a really long time; what did you ask for?"

Once they had finished their visit and moved a distance away from the file of worshippers, he posed this question to Mahiru, who had prayed at some length. She had looked like a model going through all the motions of a shrine visit. After ringing the bell, she had pressed her hands together for nearly twice as long as Amane. He had been captivated by how elegantly she had offered her prayers, but he also wondered what she had to pray for.

"Good health."

"An incredibly safe choice."

It was very typical of Mahiru.

She didn't want for very much, so Amane had wondered what she might have asked for, but it was so predictable choice that her answer was kind of anticlimactic.

"That, and—"

"And?"

"…And to be able to keep spending peaceful days together, just like we have been."

Another very typical petition.

It was just the sort of thing that Mahiru, who didn't much care for excitement or change, would pray for. It was very fitting, as she prized peace and quiet.

"We won't get much of that while my mom's around, though."

"That's something we can enjoy for what it is."

Is it, though...?

Amane wasn't sure, but Mahiru seemed to be enjoying herself, so he didn't argue and just took Mahiru's hand with a gentle smile.

They hadn't yet entirely extracted themselves from the crowd, and Amane was sure to find himself in trouble if he let Mahiru trip and fall now. He could see his parents waiting a short distance away, having already finished their own visit to the shrine. That was why Amane was holding her hand, he told himself. Mahiru's eyelashes fluttered, and she kept her eyes cast downward, looking embarrassed, but she squeezed Amane's hand back.

"You two, over here!"

His mother's voice was bright and clear, easy to distinguish among the crowd.

Following her words, the two of them headed over to Amane's parents. Shihoko's eyes went wide when she saw them, then she pressed a hand over her smiling mouth.

"Oh my, my!"

"What?"

"You're just holding hands so naturally."

It wasn't until she spelled it out that he realized what a mistake it was to hold Mahiru's hand in front of his mother. This was the kind of thing that couples did, wasn't it? He didn't appreciate Shihoko's suspicions and hated always being on the receiving end of her smirking grins.

©Hanekoto

"…It's obviously so we don't lose sight of each other. Plus, it's easy for her to trip, wearing a kimono."

"He's right. It's difficult to walk in a kimono, and he's doing the right thing by escorting her. I do the same thing for you, Shihoko dear," Amane's father agreed. In a single smooth motion, he grasped his wife's hand.

Amane's life would be easier if he were able to take a girl's hand as smoothly as his father could, but he knew it was impossible given his personality, so he was secretly grateful that Mahiru had been frank about taking his hand instead.

Feeling relieved that his mother's attention was occupied, Amane tried to gently let go of Mahiru's hand, but she wouldn't relax her grip.

He could tell from the way she squeezed that she had no intention of separating, so he quietly asked her what was wrong, but there was no answer. Her delicate fingers simply held tightly to his.

"Mahiru, Mahiru sweetie, we were thinking of going to buy some hot drinks. Would you like sweet red bean soup—or sweet sake?"

"Oh, I'll take red bean soup, please."

His mother's interruption spoiled any hope of asking Mahiru further questions or of getting his hand back.

"How about you, Amane dear?"

"…All right, I'll have sweet sake."

"Coming right up."

As long as Mahiru doesn't hate this, I guess it's fine, right?

Amane tried to calm the fluttering in his chest as he adjusted his hand in hers.

Before long, Shihoko returned from the concessions stand and handed everyone their drinks. At this point, it would have been incredibly awkward for them to continue holding hands, so Mahiru let go, and Amane got the chance to catch his breath.

His parents were smiling at each other gently as they enjoyed their sweet sake.

They weren't quite off in their own world, but they were getting flirty, so Amane had no desire to speak to them at the moment and instead focused on drinking his own sweet sake.

Sweet sake like this was said to be so nutritious it was like having an IV drip, and as the rich sweetness of the fermented rice spread through him, he unintentionally let out a sigh that was a mix of astonishment and relief.

Amane didn't usually care much for sweets, though he did rather like red bean paste, so he had also been tempted to choose the red bean soup. However, he had gone with the sake because it felt more appropriate for New Year's, and he was confident that it had been the right choice.

When he glanced over at Mahiru, he saw her sipping her sweet red bean soup from a paper cup with a calm expression. She made it look absolutely delicious, and suddenly he regretted his decision.

I wonder if I can get her to give me a sip?

He was gazing at her and wondering if he could get some if he asked, when Mahiru noticed him looking and tilted her head quizzically. Her hair decoration swayed rhythmically with her graceful movements.

"Is the sweet red bean soup any good?" Amane asked.

"It's delicious," she said, nodding.

"Could I try some?"

Mahiru looked startled by his question. It was almost comical how quickly she straightened up.

"Ah, s-sure you can, but…"

She couldn't hide how flustered she was, glancing up at him timidly.

"If you don't want me to, it's fine…"

"It's...it's not that I don't want you to, but...well—"

"Well?"

"N-no, nothing, it's fine. Here. Could I have some of your sake, too?"

"S-sure."

Mahiru quickly seized his cup. She seemed suddenly very agitated for some reason. Amane accepted her cup of red bean soup.

In it was a thick liquid that was certainly bean-colored.

When he brought the cup to his lips, the unique fragrance of sweet red beans wafted gently over him and filled his nose as a rich flavor spread over his tongue. Amane didn't have much of a sweet tooth, so even the slight sweetness of the bean soup seemed strong to him.

It was delicious and vividly brought to mind thoughts of how well sweet red bean paste paired with bitter green tea.

Since Mahiru seemed to have a thing for sweets, he thought this soup was probably just perfect for her tastes.

When he glanced over at Mahiru, perhaps because she had sipped the sweet sake, her cheeks were slightly flushed. She looked almost anxious.

"You don't like it?"

"That's not it... Amane, you made such a big deal out of sharing a piece of cake. Why doesn't this bother you?"

"...Ah."

That was when he realized why Mahiru had reacted the way she did. Amane froze in place.

We're not feeding each other, but I guess this is still an indirect kiss, huh?

His attention had been focused on the sweet red bean soup, and he had inadvertently suggested that they share an indirect kiss. He may not have realized it, but there could be no doubt that he had put

Mahiru on the spot. That must have been why she had acted the way she had.

"S-sorry. That was really thoughtless. I'm sure you hated it..."

"Wh-why are you always like that, Amane? I was just... I was embarrassed, okay? That was all."

"I— I'll be more careful in the future. Sorry."

Whatever she might have been feeling, it was a fact that he had put her on the spot. Amane bowed his head slightly, and Mahiru waved her hand in front of her face frantically.

"R-really, I'm not worried about it!"

"Are you sure? Well, I'm sorry anyway. I shouldn't treat you the same way as my other friends."

Itsuki and Chitose were the type of people who didn't care about that stuff and would take sips of Amane's drinks and bites of his food and insist it was fine because they were friends.

Itsuki was the same sex as Amane, and Chitose was the opposite sex, but he had never looked at either of them with the slightest romantic interest, so it didn't really feel like an indirect kiss when they shared food. He just got irritated when they stole his snacks.

But with Mahiru, it was obviously different. He was in the wrong for not realizing that sooner.

"Do Itsuki and Chitose usually do things like that?"

"Y-yeah, I mean, we're friends, after all..."

"Is that so?"

Mahiru nodded, wearing a complex expression that could have been either comprehension or consternation. Then she lowered her gaze back down to the sweet sake and raised the cup to her lips again.

"...I suppose, Amane, that you and I are friends, too, so it's fine."

"Y-yeah...but you drank it all, didn't you?"

Mahiru's cheeks flushed even though there was no alcohol in the drink. "Th-there wasn't much left!" She turned away sharply.

In retaliation, Amane gulped down what was left of Mahiru's sweet red bean soup. He'd expected it to have gotten cold, but it was somehow still hot and seemed even sweeter than before.

"Mahiru dear, you're such a good cook!"

By the time they made it back from the shrine visit, it was already evening. Mahiru had changed clothes and begun her usual dinner preparations, but…Amane's mother Shihoko was also in the kitchen, ostensibly to observe Mahiru's culinary skills.

His parents had decided to spend the night. Their house was several hours away by car, and they were tired. It sounded like they had been intending to stay over from the outset. Amane wished that they'd asked the guy living there first, but his father technically owned the apartment, so he knew he had no right to complain.

Luckily, he had an extra futon set just in case he ever had anyone over, so he figured they could share it. They slept in the same bed at home, so it wouldn't be that different.

"Thank you very much," Mahiru said graciously.

"Really, you're very good for a high school girl. When I was your age, there's no way I could have done all this."

"Your cooking's no match for Mahiru's now, Mom."

"Did you say something, dear?"

"Not a thing."

A low-pitched voice had come flying out of the kitchen at him, so Amane feigned innocence and huddled against the sofa. His father was relaxing on the couch next to him and chided, "Now, Amane, don't pick on your mother."

But she was always picking on him, so he felt like this was a fair turnabout.

Amane could hear his mother chatting with Mahiru in a cheerful voice.

Mahiru calmly kept up with her, unfazed by her intense energy and attention. She seemed to be getting used to the high-strung woman.

Watching from afar, Amane gazed at the two of them preparing dinner and apparently getting along well, and he let out a quiet sigh of relief.

"Your mother seems to have taken quite a liking to Miss Shiina, hasn't she?"

Amane's father was gazing at the two of them in the same way, and he looked pleased.

"Well, she's beautiful and sweet and has a nice personality, so I'm not surprised that Mom likes her."

"How about you, Amane?"

"…Oh, I mean, I think she's a nice person, and I think she's cute."

"I see."

It seemed like a casual question, but Amane's father wasn't the type of person to pry too much, so he had probably asked out of genuine curiosity. He didn't press Amane on his answer any further.

"I'm looking forward to trying this food that you enjoy every day, Amane."

"I can vouch for the taste. If Mom doesn't meddle too much, that is."

"You don't need to worry. Shihoko was the one who wanted to eat Miss Shiina's cooking, so I'm sure the most she'll do is help out a little."

"That's good, if it's true."

His mother wasn't a bad cook, but most of her dishes featured big, bold flavors, in contrast to Mahiru's subtle seasonings. Delicate flavors were his father's specialty while his mother favored quantity and ease of preparation.

Of course, that was important for a housewife who had a growing boy's appetite to satisfy, but Amane actually preferred the carefully calibrated flavors of the dishes Mahiru made. He shuddered to think of anyone meddling with Mahiru's exquisite seasonings.

Thankfully, his mother seemed to be constraining herself to being Mahiru's assistant like his father said, so he breathed a sigh of relief and continued watching the two of them cook.

"Oh yes, this is very good," Amane's father said.

There was no way that the four of them would have fit around Amane's two-person dining table, so he had pulled out the large folding desk that had been shut away in the storage room to use for dinner.

"Thank you very much." Mahiru looked relieved at Shuuto's frank assessment, and she visibly relaxed a little.

Apparently, she had never let anyone other than Amane eat her home cooking, outside of home-ec class in school, of course, and had been somewhat nervous about it...but at last that stiffness melted away once she saw Shuuto's gentle smile.

"It's really delicious," Amane's mother added. "If she can cook like this, she won't have any trouble living alone—or getting married."

Shihoko muttered quietly to herself while looking at Amane. He could feel his cheek about to twitch but forcibly maintained a neutral expression and sipped his miso soup.

The rich, dashi-infused flavor was now very familiar to him. He had really gotten used to the way Mahiru prepared her dishes and, after eating her cooking every day, had practically lost all desire to eat anything else.

"Amane, what do you think?" his mother asked.

"It's delicious, of course. Thanks for always cooking, Mahiru."

He had been planning to say as much anyway. But now that his mother had prompted him, it probably sounded like he didn't really mean it. Amane had never forgotten to tell Mahiru that her cooking was delicious every day when they ate together, but since his parents were here, he had been holding back. And that had obviously been the wrong decision.

His gratitude was no different now, but for some reason, Mahiru was restless, fidgeting uncomfortably. "...Sure," she answered in a quiet voice. Her cheeks were flushed slightly.

It was probably because his parents were there. There could be no doubt that Mahiru was feeling bashful, even if only a little. She was used to hearing Amane's appraisals of her cooking, but now three people had complimented her.

"You're awfully cute, Mahiru."

"Shihoko, don't tease."

"That's not what I meant! I was just thinking that she's a good, upstanding girl, which is so hard to find these days."

"Th-that's... It's not really..."

"Yeah, I can agree with that. Mahiru's like, really pure, you could say."

"Amane?!"

Mahiru was definitely a little naive. Her face had gone bright red once just from seeing a guy—a not particularly attractive guy—with the front of his shirt open.

"My, my, did something happen between you two while we weren't looking?"

"Nope."

"Nothing happened."

The denial practically leaped from Mahiru's mouth.

Being innocent or naive wasn't the worst thing in the world, but Mahiru seemed to hate being called those things. Amane had no plans to say anything further.

"Well, I think that they should do just as they please, as long as

Amane isn't hurting Miss Shiina, that is," Amane's father said. "Just don't tease her too much, Amane."

"I know that much."

"...Well, weren't you just teasing her?"

"Hey, it was an accurate description—"

Amane felt something strike his thigh below the table. Mahiru's face was bright red, and she was glaring in his direction.

"Sorry, sorry," he said.

A sullen expression crossed her handsome features. But that only made her look even more adorable, and Amane couldn't help but grin. He only hoped that Mahiru wouldn't stay mad at him for long.

"...You know, I can't help but feel a bit like we're looking in the mirror. What do you think, Shihoko darling?"

"I think that's just fine, Shuuto dear. Why, even our Amane is wearing an uncharacteristically gentle expression."

"What are you guys talking about over there?"

"Not a thing, dear!"

Amane could have sworn that he heard some low, conspiratorial whispers from across the table, but his parents maintained expressions of perfect innocence.

"Sorry you had to make enough for my parents, too."

After they had finished dinner and chatted pleasantly for another couple of hours, it was finally time to break up the party.

Of course, since Amane's parents would be sleeping in his living room, Mahiru was the only one going home.

Amane had sent his parents to bathe, so he was the only one who stepped outside to see Mahiru off.

There was no need for him to do so, but he wanted the chance to apologize for his mother and father, just in case.

"No, it's all right. This was fun."

"It was?"

He was glad that she didn't appear upset.

If anything, she seemed like she had enjoyed herself.

"Besides—"

"Yeah?"

"...I got a small taste of happiness, so—"

Mahiru's thin voice was almost like a sigh. She smiled but also looked very lonely all of a sudden. It was a fleeting smile, one that seemed like it could be carried away by the breeze. Amane was starting to piece together a picture of her situation at home, so he thought he recognized the faint look of yearning in her eyes.

Somehow, he couldn't leave it alone, and Amane put his palm on her head and stroked her hair.

Mahiru looked up at Amane in surprise, but she didn't seem to hate it.

"Wh-what are you doing?"

"Nothing."

"It's not nothing... My hair's all messed up."

"You're getting in the bath anyway, right?"

"I am, but—"

"...Did you hate it?"

"I—I didn't hate it, but...you could at least say something first."

"...Here we go."

"That's saying something *after.*"

So it's okay to touch you as long as I tell you first? Amane thought, but he knew better than to say it out loud.

"Sorry."

Mahiru let out a small sigh.

"Geez... I'm fine with it, but it's really not appropriate to rub a girl's head so casually."

"But I don't do it to anyone else..."

Amane understood that the only time it was okay to touch a person of the opposite sex was when you had a close relationship. He wasn't the kind of guy who would go around casually rubbing up against girls or anything. The closest he came to that was smacking Chitose whenever she made a terrible joke.

Amane had thought that maybe he and Mahiru had gotten close enough, so he had tentatively touched her, hoping she wouldn't hate it, but the thought wouldn't have even occurred to him if it was anyone else.

Mahiru had fallen quiet, but she hadn't shaken off his hand.

"...I'm sure you can see it," she said, "but you're the spitting image of your father, Amane. It's obvious to me, even though I've only known him a short while."

"In what sense? I really don't think I resemble him that much, either physically or with my personality."

"...You're *exactly* like him. Truly."

Mahiru sighed more heavily this time, and Amane rubbed her head again. She still didn't seem to be against it.

...Do I really resemble him that much?

Sure, they had once or twice been mistaken for brothers far apart in age, but Amane felt like he had a completely different energy from his father. Their personalities, too, while not exact opposites, nevertheless were quite different.

What could she have meant by saying that he was just like his father, despite such clear differences?

Any number of doubts welled up in Amane's mind, but Mahiru must not have intended to say anything further. Her eyes narrowed a bit, and she left the matter alone.

After stroking her hair a bit more, Amane pulled back, and Mahiru seemed to suddenly snap back to her senses. She peered up at Amane, slightly flustered.

"What, you wanted me to keep going?" he asked teasingly.

Mahiru flushed red again. "Please don't mock me," she said quietly, so he decided to call it a day.

Apparently, she was in a bad mood now, for she made no attempt to hide the displeasure on her face as she opened the door to her own apartment and slipped inside.

For a brief moment, Amane regretted his actions, wondering if he had overdone it a little, when Mahiru cracked her door open and peeked out at him.

"Amane."

Her cheeks were still pink, and her voice sounded peevish but with a slight fawning tone to it somehow.

"What?"

"...You're a dummy."

Just as suddenly, Mahiru shut the door.

...Well, that makes two of us, I guess.

Wasn't it Mahiru's fault that his heart was suddenly leaping in his chest?

Amane sighed quietly, then leaned against the wall of the unheated corridor, trying to let the sudden burning in his chest cool a bit. That was the moment he noticed he could see his breath in the frosty air.

A short while after Amane had said goodnight to Mahiru and returned to his apartment, his parents finished their bath. When Amane looked up from the TV toward the sound of approaching slippers, he saw them standing there in their nightclothes, casually holding hands.

Well, I guess that comes naturally if you've already taken a bath together.

"We've had our bath, Amane. It's your turn."

"Sure... Wait, how did you two manage to both fit in my tub? It's only big enough for one."

For someone living alone, this was quite a spacious, well-designed apartment, but that didn't mean the bathtub was especially large. It certainly wasn't big enough for a full-grown man and woman to sit together comfortably.

"Oh no, it's fine! There's no problem if you get in close together. Right, Shuuto dear?"

His mother smiled and drew closer to her husband, and his father nodded in agreement with a gentle smile. They had already been married for nearly twenty years, but the two of them still acted like newlyweds. Amane could do nothing but smile bitterly.

"As loving as always, I see."

"Are you jealous?"

"Not really. I can relax better in the bath alone anyway."

"What about Mahiru...?"

"All right, listen up. Nothing is going on with her."

He didn't understand why his mother wanted so badly to hook him up with Mahiru.

Well, it wasn't a total mystery, since she'd been joking about wanting Mahiru for a daughter-in-law since the day they'd met, but Amane was certain his mother had mistaken the trust that Mahiru had in Amane for romantic affection.

"Is that so?"

"Now, now, Shihoko. Amane's at a delicate age, so let's be considerate."

"But I'm being serious..."

"Whatever you say, Mom."

Amane paid his mother's words no mind as he stood up to get ready for his bath, but he stopped when his father called his name.

"Amane." He used a serious tone, not the voice he used to chide his wife or the one that he had when he smiled. When Amane looked at him, wondering what was the matter, he was met with a soft but firm gaze.

"Amane, are you glad you moved here?"

Though he was caught by surprise, after a moment Amane quickly met his father's steady gaze with an easy smile.

"...Yeah, I am. Life got easier."

Surely his parents must have been worried about him. Worried enough to frequently come check on how he was doing and worried enough to try to see him at every opportunity.

All of it had been in order to make sure that Amane was living comfortably.

"Is that so? I'm glad."

"You don't need to worry; there's someone here who I can really rely on."

Unlike before—

He swallowed those words and kept his answer simple and clean.

His mother smiled brightly. "Oh, you must mean little Itsuki! I've never met him in person, so I wanted to go say hello, since we came all this way."

"Give it a rest, please; you're going to start something weird."

"It's not weird at all. I'll tell him how cute you were when you were little, and..."

"See, that's exactly what I'm talking about. Seriously, just stop..."

If this spilled over to Itsuki, then it was certain to reach Chitose as well. That was the one thing Amane wanted to avoid no matter what. He did not want to deal with her endless teasing or put up with her badgering him for old photos from his past.

Amane had looked remarkably like a cute little girl when he was small, and it didn't help that his mother sometimes even dressed him up in girls' clothes. If photographic evidence of *that* got out, his life would be nothing but suffering.

"But I can't help wanting to say hello, can I? He's such good friends with you, Amane."

"That's true, but—"

"I bet he's a really good boy, isn't he? He's got the Amane seal of approval, after all."

"...He's a good guy. So good that he's wasted on me."

It wasn't something he would ever say to Itsuki's face, but Amane always appreciated his friend who once took the initiative to call out in a friendly voice to a very gloomy boy who never interacted with anyone and just sat quietly on the side of the classroom listening to music.

"I'm going to take a bath."

He felt embarrassed after openly praising Itsuki, even though he wasn't there, and to disguise his discomfort, he quickly headed for his bedroom to retrieve a change of clothes.

He could hear a small chuckle behind his back, compelling Amane to escape to his room, scowling and muttering the whole way.

The following morning, when Amane went out into the living room after waking up and dressing, he found his parents already up and food on the table.

"Good morning. Breakfast is ready, so have a seat."

Amane sat down at the table, smiling slightly at his father, who called to him from the kitchen, wearing Amane's apron, which had been draped over a chair.

He had only just arrived in this apartment and had already made himself comfortable in an unfamiliar kitchen, probably because he was so used to doing the cooking. At home, Amane's parents took turns preparing meals, so Amane was also used to seeing his father in an apron, and there was nothing unusual about it.

Amane's mother was already waiting impatiently at the table. She probably wanted to help, but his father had likely insisted that she leave it to him.

Amane also considered helping and got as far as standing up from his seat only to see his father bring out steaming hot rice and miso soup on a tray, immediately taking the wind out of Amane's sails.

"Thanks, Dad."

"Don't mention it. Anyway, Miss Shiina was kind enough to pack yesterday's leftovers into containers, so I just heated that up, cooked some rice, then made miso soup and rolled omelets."

Eat a proper breakfast was practically a motto in the Fujimiya household, so they never skipped their morning meal.

Amane's father had happily incorporated the leftovers into the menu, but if they hadn't had them, there was little doubt he would have whipped up something.

With a smile, Shuuto placed the rice and miso soup in front of each of them.

Amane's attention was drawn to his father's rolled omelets, which he hadn't tasted in a while, and before he knew it, the table was set, and his father had taken his own seat.

"All right, let's get to it, shall we?"

"Certainly. Thank you, dear."

"Thanks for the meal."

Everyone expressed their gratitude, and then Amane reached with his chopsticks for the rolled omelets in front of him.

This was the first time Amane had eaten his father's cooking since he went home for summer break, so he was looking forward to the nostalgia of it as he took his first bite and slowly chewed.

The flavor of the dashi, the hint of sweetness, the slightly under-cooked egg—it tasted like home—yet at the same time, Amane found something slightly lacking.

"Is something the matter?"

His father seemed to have noticed Amane chewing with a serious expression and sounded concerned.

"Mm…no, it's nothing."

"Did I maybe mess up the seasonings?"

"N-no, that's not it; it's good, but…I was just thinking that the flavor is different from the way that Mahiru always makes omelets."

"Ah, so that's it."

He hadn't eaten his father's cooking for almost half a year, so even though it should have been familiar, he was actually more accustomed to Mahiru's cooking after eating it every day. Even Amane was surprised.

Of course, that wasn't to say that his father's cooking was bad or anything, just that Mahiru's seasonings were more to Amane's tastes. But even so, he felt somewhat self-conscious about the fact that his tongue had adapted so well to Mahiru's cooking, when he had only met her a few months earlier.

"You've really fallen for Miss Shiina, haven't you?" his father asked.

"For her cooking, yeah."

"Hey, now," his mother crowed. "Are you saying you're not interested in Mahiru herself, then?"

"No one is saying that, and I do not intend to fall for such a leading question."

Amane was not about to let his mother steer the conversation in that direction again.

Shihoko frowned—obviously, her aim had been exactly as Amane expected. Amane snorted through his nose and refused to take the bait.

His parents departed before lunch.

Both of them apparently had work the next day, so Amane had suggested that it would be hard on them if they didn't get home early and rest. They had a long drive ahead of them, which would of course be exhausting, so it was better if they hurried up and got going.

"But I wanted to talk more with my dear Mahiru and meet Itsuki...," his mother muttered quietly after stepping out the door into the building's hallway.

"Then do that stuff next time... Besides, you'll have to make an appointment to see Itsuki. He doesn't have a lot of free time."

"All right, you set it up for me then, Amane."

"If I feel like it."

It was obvious to everyone that Amane had no intention of doing anything of the sort. His mother grew sullen, but Amane's father soothed her—and more or less restored her good spirits.

As Amane was watching his parents, the door to the next-door apartment quietly creaked open. From the narrow crack, he could see a flash of golden hair and Mahiru's face peeking out.

She must have come out because she had heard his mother talking. For better or worse, his mother's voice traveled quite well.

"Oh, perfect, I was just thinking about coming to say good-bye!"

Both of Amane's parents noticed Mahiru and moved over to stand in front of her apartment as she slipped on a pair of shoes and stepped out into the hallway. Amane's mother was wearing a big smile and seemed determined to get as close to Mahiru as possible. Mahiru shrunk back but didn't retreat entirely.

"Are you two leaving already?"

"I wish we weren't. Really, we'd like to stay another day or two, but we have work."

"Things would be different if we had come up a little bit earlier, but...this is all the time we have."

Mahiru smiled placidly at Amane's parents.

"Well, there's always next time," his mother said. "Although, next time it's Amane's turn to come to us."

"Yeah, yeah. I'll be home for summer vacation."

Amane could feel his mother's gaze bearing down on him. He knew right away she was hoping that he would bring Mahiru along with him.

Still, he couldn't help but wonder if that might be a good idea. She apparently spent her school breaks alone, after all. *Maybe she wouldn't be so opposed to the idea*, he thought idly.

"You really have no charm at all, Amane," his mother said. "Isn't that right, Mahiru?"

"Uh, I… I'm not sure how to—"

"Come now, Shihoko, don't put her on the spot," Amane's father chided. "…Though, it's true that Amane has gotten less up front about various things as he's gotten older, hasn't he?"

Amane had no allies here, so he silently pretended to ignore his parents. Shuuto turned to Mahiru with a gentle smile that was different than Shihoko's.

"As you can see, our Amane has a hard time expressing his feelings, but if you look closely, you can tell that he's a kindhearted young man. I would be very happy if you would continue to be a good friend to him."

"Ugh, I'm right here, you know. This is so embarrassing…"

His father had praised him, but Amane felt more like he had been goaded by an enemy than supported by an ally.

He certainly didn't think of himself as a particularly kindhearted person. He just showed the people close to him the respect and affection he thought they deserved. It felt wrong to have that confused with kindness.

Awkwardly trying to find anywhere else to look, Amane glanced over at Mahiru and saw her blink quickly and smile.

"…I've always thought that Amane is an honest and kind person. So much so that I'm the one who should be asking for his continued friendship."

"Well, that's wonderful. That puts my mind at ease."

Amane wanted to make a quip about his father's mind being at ease, but he was so shaken by what Mahiru had said that he couldn't think of anything. It was so embarrassing to hear her describe him that way. He couldn't even look at her.

His mother laughed as she watched him squirm, but Amane couldn't even respond. He could only bite his lip in tortured silence.

"You don't really need to flatter me, you know."

After Amane's parents had finally departed, he spoke to Mahiru in a quiet voice as they stood alone in the hallway.

Amane had made that remark to relieve the awkward atmosphere somewhat, but for some reason, Mahiru raised her eyebrows and stared at him.

Her expression was calm, but there was a subtle edge to it that he found intimidating.

"Do I seem like the type to say empty words I don't mean?"

"Well, you wouldn't lie to me—but maybe in front of my parents?"

She seemed to object to him calling it flattery.

Mahiru huffed and then let out a sigh of exasperation.

"...Now see here, I trust you because I think you have a good heart, and I really do like spending time with you. I promise: I was not trying to flatter you."

"O-oh..."

Amane felt the heat rushing to his face. Hearing her talk so candidly was terribly embarrassing. Fortunately, Mahiru did not seem to notice his unease, and he nodded meekly.

Mahiru seemed satisfied. "As long as you understand. Well, I suppose I'll get started on lunch."

Apparently, Mahiru was going to fix him lunch today, just as she had done every day of the New Year's holiday. Feeling a mixture of gratitude and shame, Amane looked down at Mahiru's golden hair as she placed a hand on the door to his apartment.

Someone she can trust, huh...? That's what I was gonna say.

Mahiru ignored the fact that Amane thought she was an angel. To her, he was an ordinary neighbor. But she trusted him. That was what he was most grateful for.

"I'm so glad I moved here."

Mahiru must have heard his quiet mumbling, because she turned around and asked, "Did you say something?"

"No, nothing," Amane said quickly, following her into his apartment.

Chapter 4

A New Semester

A new school semester had started, but not much had changed.

Everyone seemed to have spent the winter vacation relaxing, so there weren't any major developments the way summer vacation could sometimes bring. The usual cast of characters was back, and no one had undergone a drastic image change or anything.

Amane was seated at his desk, quietly gazing at a classroom that was somewhat more boisterous than usual, when a shadow loomed over him.

"Yo, Amane, what's good."

"Thanks, can't complain."

It was Itsuki, who had entered the classroom from behind Amane's seat. Itsuki was no exception and had also remained the same.

Amane hadn't seen him since Christmas, but he was wearing the same flippant smile as always.

"So did you have a good holiday?"

"...P-pretty much, yeah."

"C'mon, you're holding something back. Was there some kind of...progress?"

"What? Look, it's not like that. And just so you know, nothing happened."

That wasn't actually true, of course. But Amane wouldn't dream of telling Itsuki that Mahiru had stayed over at his place, even if it had been an accident.

He knew the moment he told Itsuki, Itsuki was guaranteed to tell Chitose, and it wasn't hard to imagine that the two of them would start teasing and poking fun at him first chance they got.

Aside from that incident, all that had happened over the break was his parents coming over and their communal visit to the shrine, which surely fell into the category of *nothing*.

"…Hmm?"

"I didn't really do anything."

"Well, I guess I shouldn't be surprised, but…"

Amane found Itsuki's rather triumphant smile pretty irritating but decided that responding would just encourage him, so he let it go.

He looked around the classroom, hunting for some topic that would let him change the subject…but nothing was particularly new or notable.

As always, the girls were standing around Yuuta Kadowaki, the so-called prince of their grade. As always, the boys in the room were openly jealous, even though Yuuta himself wore a slightly troubled expression.

"That dynamic hasn't changed one bit," Amane remarked.

"Yeah, good ol' Yuuta. Same old spectacle, huh?"

In the end, Amane, who considered it none of his business, and Itsuki, who had a girlfriend and wasn't interested in other girls, smiled wryly at Yuuta's popularity and continued scanning their familiar surroundings.

"Come to think of it, I heard that Shiina might have a boyfriend, you know."

A group of several girls formed nearby, and Amane could hear what they were talking about. He suddenly stiffened.

"Oh, Risa told me, yeah. She went on a shrine visit and saw her holding hands with a boy."

"Yeah, I heard! Shiina has never been swayed by anyone before, but maybe that was because she had a boyfriend?"

"Sounds like he was a really cool-looking guy, but Risa said she's never seen him before. He must be from another school."

Somehow, it felt like the attention of the whole classroom shifted to the girls' conversation. Even Yuuta seemed to be looking over and perking up his ears.

Only Itsuki was looking at Amane.

"Hey, Amane."

"I know nothing."

"I didn't even ask you anything yet."

"I'm not involved."

"Sure."

Itsuki smiled knowingly at Amane, who had shut him down in a quiet voice, then flicked Amane's bangs up and out of the way.

"Say, you always hide your face, but it's not too shabby."

"I can't take that as anything but mockery when you say it."

Itsuki could be a real prankster, and he never seemed to take much of anything seriously, and he was definitely a good-looking guy himself, so when he told Amane that he had an attractive face, it sounded decidedly sarcastic.

Amane knew he was an average-looking guy at best, and it made him uncomfortable to hear other people talking about his appearance.

He slapped Itsuki's hand away from his bangs and scowled, but his friend only grinned.

"That's just the sort of guy you are."

"Shut up."

"Well, can't say it's out of character."

Amane was still acting cold, and Itsuki grinned at him without even a hint of anger.

"There's a rumor going around school."

They were still seated across from each other at the dining table after dinner when he shared the news, and Mahiru's face stiffened, as if she already knew exactly what he was talking about.

Mahiru was sure to have the most trouble from the situation.

As far as Amane could tell from what he'd heard, he had yet to be identified as the mystery man, but even so, it must have been exhausting, having everyone suddenly asking her about having a boyfriend.

That must have been why Mahiru was moving stiffly and stepping just a little wearily when she came over to Amane's apartment that day.

"...It's all right, because no one knows that it was you, Amane, but everyone's really taken it the wrong way. This is going to be a difficult misunderstanding to clear up."

"Is holding your hand enough to turn someone into your boyfriend?"

"I don't know. For the time being, I've been strongly denying everything, telling people that the boy was just an acquaintance. Now we have to wait for the rumor to die down."

"Mm, well, I guess there's nothing else we can do, huh?"

Obviously, people would think less of Mahiru if they thought that she was dating a guy like Amane, so he hoped that the rumors would burn out quickly. She was clearly stressed, having person after person question her about a maybe-boyfriend.

At the same time, Amane felt an uneasy tinge of regret and embarrassment whenever he heard the rumors circulating, so he also wanted to put the whole thing behind them.

Amane sighed heavily, while Mahiru just quietly cast her eyes downward.

"...Did we really look that much like sweethearts?" Mahiru suddenly asked.

"I wonder. To be honest, I can't really see you ever going out with a guy like me. You'd definitely go for a smarter, more attractive guy, so I think even if I saw us standing side by side, I'd assume we were simply acquaintances rather than boyfriend and girlfriend."

"That's not true."

"Huh?"

Mahiru had answered him in a stronger voice than expected. When he turned to look at her again, she was not wearing the worried face she'd been making earlier. Instead, for some reason, Mahiru seemed a little...angry. She had a determined look about her.

"Amane, your assessment of yourself is quite low, but it's not accurate. I think that you're a very well-balanced person. You're kind and considerate and gentlemanly, so I think you've got a very good personality. And when you got all dressed up, I think you looked really nice, too."

Her words were far too kind. Amane could scarcely believe that she was talking about him. His face began to turn bright red. He never would have imagined that Mahiru thought so highly of him, and she was saying these things so earnestly that it made him feel awkward to be on the receiving end of her praise.

Apparently, he was not the only one feeling a bit awkward. Midway through, Mahiru's voice had begun to tremble, but she still looked Amane directly in the eye, making sure that he fully understood that this was her honest opinion. Of course, that didn't make it any less embarrassing.

"Oh r-really...? Um, o-okay, thanks."

"S-so, um, well...don't put yourself down so much."

"Y-yeah…"

Amane didn't feel any urge to argue with her. It was obvious that she wouldn't hear it.

Mahiru's cheeks were tinged with red as she squirmed and shifted, looking at the floor. Amane groaned. He wasn't sure what to do, either. Anything had to be better than doing nothing while the frustration and humiliation kept bubbling up inside him.

"…Uh, I'm gonna go wash the dishes."

"O-okay."

At the moment, a tactical retreat seemed like the best play. Avoid and escape. Staying here to watch Mahiru tremble in shame was bad for his heart.

As he took two deep breaths and then stood up from the table and gathered the dishes and carried them to the sink, Mahiru sank into the living room sofa and buried her face in a cushion. She was acting as if she was the one in anguish over getting unexpected compliments.

"If you're that embarrassed," Amane grumbled to himself, "maybe you shouldn't have said anything." But he felt as if a slight weight had been lifted off his chest by Mahiru's words. The whole thing had been heart-wrenching, for sure, but also a bit of a relief.

Even though it was winter, Amane decided to wash the dishes with cold water. He hoped the icy shock would help clear his mind.

"Hey, hey, Amane? Can I borrow the angel?"

The phone call from Chitose came in the evening, three days after the new semester had started.

Normally, they would talk through a messaging app, but for some unknown reason, she actually called him. And she was asking about Mahiru. Amane was really confused.

Chitose asked to borrow Mahiru, but Mahiru's not mine to lend out, so if Chitose wants some of her time, she had better ask her herself.

"Don't ask me. Ask her."

"Is she there with you?"

"…She is, but—"

"All right, ask her if she wants to hang out together tomorrow after school."

"Ask her yourself!"

He briefly wondered if she didn't have Mahiru's contact information, but then he remembered at Christmastime when Chitose had been so busy messing with Mahiru that she had completely forgotten to exchange numbers with the girl.

So she must have decided that the best way to get to Mahiru was through Amane, who definitely had Mahiru's contact information and could often be found right beside her, too. He could understand the thought process, but he wanted to tell her that he wasn't a carrier pigeon, delivering messages back and forth like it was his job.

For the time being, he decided that she had better talk to Mahiru directly, so he handed the phone over to Mahiru, who was sitting next to him looking confused, and told her, "Chitose wants to talk to you."

Mahiru looked perplexed but dutifully took the smartphone and held it up to her ear as Amane leaned back in his seat.

"Mahiru here… Huh, tomorrow? S-sure, I don't have any particular plans, but…"

Amane smiled mischievously as he watched Mahiru's troubled expression.

I bet Chitose's putting the pressure on her by talking a mile a minute like always.

Mahiru didn't look upset or anything. She just seemed earnestly surprised by the sudden proposal and unsure how to handle it.

She was shooting glances over at Amane, so he told her, "I'll leave it up to your judgment. She wants to hang out with you, not me."

Even Mahiru hung out with friends sometimes, but she preferred to come home after a few hours and spend her time in the kitchen.

Amane thought that she could do with an excuse to go relax a bit, though he wasn't entirely sure that hanging out with Chitose really lent itself to relaxation.

"S-sure... Um, in that case, I think I'll accept your invitation, but..."

Perhaps Amane's assurance had been the deciding factor. When she told Chitose as much, the happy "Yay!!" from the other end of the phone line was clearly audible, and Mahiru reflexively pulled the phone away from her ear.

Amane caught Mahiru's eye and gave her a knowing smile. Chitose could be...a lot to handle. Mahiru also smiled, looking a bit nervous but also relieved and even happy.

When Chitose finally settled down, Mahiru returned the phone to her ear. Amane watched them chat for another moment or two before Mahiru eventually hung up.

"Thank you very much," she said politely. "Here's your phone back."

Their conversation had apparently reached a resolution, and tomorrow she would be joining Chitose on some excursion.

"Well, that was sudden. Then again, that's how Chitose always operates."

"W-well, I certainly was surprised."

"She's not a bad person. She can just be a little forceful."

Amane knew that was quite the understatement. Chitose usually meant well, but she could definitely be pushy.

Mahiru wore a troubled smile, as if she already knew that, but she didn't seem upset, so that was good, Amane thought. He'd always found it a little sad how few people got along with their buddies' girlfriends.

"Go have fun tomorrow; don't worry about me."

"All right."

"…Oh, that's right—"

"What?"

There was one thing that Amane had to warn her about.

"If she starts harassing you or makes you uncomfortable, feel free to give her a smack. You don't have to hold back. That girl is exactly like my mom—she loves cute things, so she's almost certainly going to get handsy with a beauty like you."

Amane had managed to keep Chitose in check before, but now he was a little worried to be sending Mahiru off alone with her. Mahiru was undeniably beautiful—she turned heads wherever she went. He knew she had to be careful about getting hit on by strangers, but Chitose was another matter. Yes, he had relied on Chitose's keen insight on the occasion of Mahiru's birthday, but he also knew that when it came to cute things, the girl just couldn't help herself. Amane felt it was necessary to at least warn Mahiru about Chitose's wandering hands.

"Now, I don't think she's going to bother you too much, but if you only give her a halfhearted rejection, she's bound to get excited and pounce you, so be careful." Amane noticed that Mahiru's lips were pressed tightly together so he cocked his head quizzically and asked, "Hey, what's up?"

"…Nothing at all."

Mahiru quietly averted her eyes.

On the day that Mahiru was supposed to hang out with Chitose, Amane hurried home and spent some quiet time alone for the first time in a while.

Recently, he and Mahiru had been spending pretty much every day together, especially with her making his lunch sometimes, so this was almost like a holiday for Amane.

Of course, he was happy that they were together so often…but sometimes it was nice to have space to himself like this, too.

The seat beside him felt a little cold, though.

Man, I really got used to having Mahiru around, huh?

Only a few months had passed since they'd first met, and he was already taking her presence for granted. Amane felt like they'd gotten very close, more like two people who'd known each other for years, rather than months. He figured that they must be quite compatible.

Personally, Amane really liked where they were in their relationship—they were close enough to enjoy the time they spent together without stepping on each other's toes.

The only problem was, he liked it so much that he didn't want to let go.

Man, I'm simpleminded.

Amane wasn't the kind of guy to come out and passionately declare his love, but he couldn't deny that his feelings for Mahiru went far beyond those of a neighbor and a friend. At the same time, he refused to allow himself to develop any serious romantic interest in her. If he let the scales tip any further, he didn't think he would be able to see Mahiru as a friend anymore. Amane was aware of the tension in his heart, and it made him deeply uneasy.

That's why he took his romantic feelings and stuffed them deep down in his gut where nobody would see them.

Mahiru would only be troubled by his affection, he knew. She cared about him in her own way, but it was obvious that she was not in love with him or anything like that. There was no way that she would ever fall for a loser like him.

Sure, she sometimes said nice things about him, but that didn't mean she thought about him that way, and if he tried to complicate their relationship by taking it in a direction that she didn't like, it would only make things awkward.

Amane turned to look out the window, hoping to get away from the squirming uneasiness in his chest.

It was winter, so the days ended early, and a curtain of utter darkness had fallen over the sky. It was just past six o'clock, but it already seemed late at night.

Mahiru was with Chitose, so she wasn't going to be out too late, but even so, he felt a little anxious at the idea of two good-looking high school girls walking around alone in this darkness.

When will you two be done?

When he sent this message to Chitose, who always kept her smartphone close, he got a reply right away.

We're saying good-bye soon.

Feeling relieved that Chitose wasn't going to keep them out all night, Amane sent another message asking when they expected to get to the station. Then he stood up from the sofa and headed for the bathroom.

I think I have a little hair wax left over from the other day.

He wasn't all that interested in styling his hair, but if he was planning to go meet Mahiru in public, it was the least he could do.

If he was being honest, getting dressed up was a huge pain, but Amane's parents had taught him how to make himself presentable. Surely he could reproduce the hairstyle from memory.

When he looked in the mirror, Amane saw his usual gloomy self staring back at him. He popped open the hair wax, confident that he could transform the uncouth, unfashionable youth standing before him.

It was the middle of winter, and on top of that, the sun had set, so the temperature had dipped quite low.

After considering both warmth and fashion, Amane decided on a light-gray sweater and navy blue peacoat, paired with fleece-lined black skinny jeans, but even so, he was undeniably cold. He could only imagine how cold Mahiru must have felt in only her school uniform and jacket.

Even though Mahiru wore thick tights during the winter, her uniform's skirt, its length determined by school regulations, still looked downright freezing to him. He wanted to tell her it'd be better to wear sweatpants underneath it.

Some of the girls he walked past were wearing even shorter skirts. Amane was keenly aware of the tremendous lengths some people would go to in pursuit of fashion.

As these thoughts bounced around in his mind, he nestled the lower half of his face in the scarf he had received from Mahiru and hurried to the nearest station.

Apparently, the girls had taken the train to a big shopping complex. The station was within walking distance of Amane's apartment, and according to Chitose, the train should be arriving any moment, so he had probably shown up at just the right time.

As Amane walked, his freshly styled hair was blown about a bit by the wind, but not badly enough to mess it up.

If it had gotten too ruffled, of course he would have had to stop to fix it, however reluctant he might be. Amane was quickly gaining a newfound respect for anyone who strove to be fashionable every day.

He was walking silently, lost in his own thoughts, when the station came into view.

Considering the direction of the apartment complex, Mahiru should come out of this exit, so if I wait nearby, I'm sure I'll see her.

He leaned against the wall near the exit and waited, checking the time. Before long, a girl with familiar blond hair came out of the gates.

"Mahiru!" he called out to her.

Recognizing his voice, Mahiru turned to look—and the moment she laid eyes on Amane, she practically froze.

"Ah...what? Wh-why?"

She was obviously surprised by his appearance. Chitose must have told her that he was coming to meet her, but she clearly hadn't expected him to show up looking like he had during their New Year's shrine visit.

But Amane hadn't even entertained the idea of coming out with his usual sloppy appearance and normal hairdo. He would be in trouble if someone identified him as the mystery man, so if he was going to accompany Mahiru in public, he needed to dress up a bit. He had to disguise himself, of course, but he also felt like he should look decent if he was going to be seen with her in public.

"What, did you think I couldn't dress myself? I can't exactly come meet you at the station in my normal clothes, now can I?"

"...I suppose not, but—"

"Does it look bad? I checked myself in the mirror, but maybe it's weird..."

He had chosen an ordinary, safe outfit and tried to style his hair like it had been on the day of the shrine visit, so Amane had hoped that he didn't look too strange. But now he realized that it probably looked all wrong to anybody with real taste.

He could feel people's gazes flicker over him from time to time, so there was a good chance that he did look weird after all. It was a bit of a shock to realize that he looked unfashionable despite trying his best.

But Mahiru shook her head, appearing flustered. "It looks good," she reassured him, and Amane felt himself breathe a sigh of relief.

"I'm glad you think so. Look, it's already dark, right? It would be dangerous to walk home alone."

"...I kn-know that, but—"

"I guess you probably didn't want me to come meet you after all. Well, if you don't want to walk together, I can walk a little ways ahead, and you can just follow me, I guess…"

"I—I never said that. I, umm…really do appreciate it."

"Of course."

Amane was happy to hear that she didn't object to him being there. He pulled a hand out of his pocket and offered it to her. Timidly, she pressed her palm into his. Maybe it was because of the cold weather, but her hand felt much chillier than he expected.

"So cold. What happened to your gloves?"

"I washed them, so they're still drying. And anyway, where are yours?"

"I just stuck my hands in my pockets."

He couldn't scold her too much, since he'd also forgotten to wear gloves, a lesson he should have learned as a child.

Amane didn't say anything further and simply kept her dainty hand nestled in his palm. It felt incredibly delicate compared to his.

"…So warm…," Mahiru mumbled quietly, and her eyes twinkled happily as she smiled.

Amane felt his heart wrench when he saw her innocent expression, but he refused to let it show and kept his attention solely focused on her small hand in his as he casually slipped Mahiru's schoolbag, as well as several shopping bags she'd acquired on her outing, over his shoulder.

Mahiru glanced up at him but didn't say anything.

"What is it?" he asked.

Abruptly, Mahiru turned away. Her ears and cheeks were slightly red, probably from the cold, he thought.

"Come on, let's go home. Do you want to stop at the convenience store on the way? The pork buns are good this time of year."

"…I'm happy with a sweet bean bun."

"You sure do like sweets… What are we doing about dinner?"

"I've marinated some eggs and prepared some *char siu* pork and bamboo shoots, so we're having ramen."

"Ramen is perfect on a cold day, huh?"

"Yes, it is."

Amane hadn't looked in the refrigerator, so he was pleasantly surprised to hear the evening's menu. Sure, the soup and noodles would be prepackaged, but Mahiru had made the toppings by hand. Amane's mouth started to water as he imagined the thick slices of pork and perfectly seasoned soft-boiled eggs.

They were sure to hit the spot on a chilly winter evening.

"…I wonder if I'll be able to eat a whole bowl of ramen after a bean bun?"

"Well then, how about you give me half? That way, you can probably finish both."

"…Okay."

For some reason, Mahiru looked a little embarrassed, so Amane smiled slightly and squeezed her hand just a little.

"Shiina was spotted with another mystery man!"

The following day, Itsuki shot him a hard look. "Not only are the rumors still spreading, somebody added fuel to the fire. What're ya gonna do, Amane?"

Amane turned away sharply. "Hell if I know…"

Chapter 5

The Angel in Poor Health

It happened on a Friday, on one of the last days of January.

"...Hmm?"

Amane returned to the living room after cleaning up dinner, but when he looked at Mahiru, he noticed that her cheeks were unusually red.

At first, he thought that maybe the thermostat was set too high, but it was on the same temperature as always, and Mahiru wasn't wearing particularly warm clothing, either. When he looked closely, he saw that her expression seemed distant and kind of unfocused. Her breathing was also shallower than usual. All signs pointed to her being sick.

When he took a moment to think about it, the weather had gotten much colder lately, and Mahiru, as an honors student, had been busy helping her teacher with some big project. On top of that, she was doing her usual housework and making dinner for the two of them. It wasn't strange at all for her to fall ill with such a workload.

Amane admonished himself for not noticing her condition earlier. He regretted not paying more attention to her.

"Mahiru, your face is red. Do you think you have a fever?"

"Of course not."

Mahiru decisively dismissed Amane's concerns. Her expression was stiff, and she shook her head, but she couldn't hide the redness in her cheeks.

Obviously, he couldn't just take her word for it, so even though he knew that it was rude to touch her without her permission, Amane gently placed the palm of his hand on Mahiru's forehead, which was usually hidden by her bangs.

As he had expected, her head was much hotter than his palm. Mahiru's typical body temperature wasn't that high compared to Amane's, so it was pretty clear she had a fever.

"You're hot as the sun."

"…No, I'm not."

"All right, how about we take your temperature and confirm it?"

"There's no need. You're worrying over nothing."

Her voice was thin and lacked her usual energy.

"Oh, come on. I can tell by looking at you that you're running a fever."

"I'm just a bit flushed."

"If that's the case, then you'll need to take your temperature and prove it."

Amane stood up and retrieved a thermometer from the first aid box on the shelf in the living room. He brought it back to Mahiru, but she turned her face away.

She either didn't want to acknowledge her fever, or she insisted on bluffing.

It was probably one or the other, but Amane couldn't really proceed until she agreed to have her temperature taken. He stood right in front of the uncooperative Mahiru and placed the thermometer firmly in her hand.

"Mahiru, either I can loosen your clothes and stick the

thermometer in your armpit, or you can take your own temperature... Which do you prefer?"

Amane put on a very serious face when he made this threat.

Mahiru let out a startled groan and turned her body toward the back of the sofa. She seemed like she had resigned herself to it, and he heard the sound of the thermometer turning on, so just to be safe, Amane also turned his back to Mahiru and waited for her to finish.

Before long, he heard another electronic beep. Amane waited for Mahiru to put her clothes back in order. When he turned around, she was looking at him, expressionless, holding the thermometer in its case.

"...Thirty-seven point two degrees Celsius. A slight fever, all right?"

"Hmm..."

"It's only a little higher than usual, and I still feel totally fine, so..."

Amane took the thermometer from Mahiru's hand and removed it from the case again. The thermometer Amane had used was the type that recorded the previously measured temperature, and when he turned it on again—sure enough, it displayed a temperature more than one whole degree higher than Mahiru had reported.

"Oh yeah? I see thirty-eight point four here."

She averted her eyes.

"Seriously, have you been running yourself ragged and letting me sit on my butt the whole time? You're taking all day tomorrow and tomorrow night off. No buts."

When Amane caught a cold, Mahiru had put him to bed and had him change into pajamas and brought him rice porridge, but he wondered how she would fare doing nothing when it was her turn.

Amane had a relatively sturdy constitution, so he'd simply gone to sleep and woken up feeling better, but if Mahiru didn't rest and kept running around, she would never recover, even from something relatively minor. Mahiru was sick, and that meant no straining herself.

However, Mahiru was still avoiding his gaze. She didn't seem likely to agree to a strict regimen of bed rest.

...So stubborn... Well, I guess there's no other way, then.

Amane extended a hand to Mahiru.

The fever was slowing her down, and it took her a moment to turn to him. Thinking that it would be just perfect if she didn't resist, Amane put his arms around Mahiru's back and under her knees and lifted her off the sofa.

Carrying her like a child, so that she had to cling tightly to him, Amane checked that he could hear the sound of jangling keys from Mahiru's pocket and headed for the door.

"Uh, A-Amane...?"

Mahiru seemed to finally realize that she was being carried, and he heard her flustered voice coming from between his arms.

When Amane stopped for a moment and looked down at her, Mahiru's cheeks were still red with fever, and she was peering up at him with confusion in her eyes.

"You're definitely going to push yourself too hard, so I'm going to keep watch until you fall asleep."

"Y-you're going to barge into a girl's bedroom?"

"If you don't like that idea, you can sleep in my room."

"...And the option for you to leave me alone...?"

"That ship sailed when you refused to rest."

Even Amane knew that no matter how close of a friend he was, going into a girl's apartment, and what's more, into her bedroom, and standing guard until she fell asleep, would be a serious invasion of her privacy. It was definitely not something he would ever even consider under normal circumstances. But after seeing the way she was acting, he was seriously worried for her health. He just knew that Mahiru

©Hanekoto

would run herself into the ground if he didn't do something. As far as he was concerned, there wasn't any other option.

Long ago, Mahiru had forced her way into his apartment, so he figured that just this once, he would employ the same forceful measures for her sake.

"Okay, which do you prefer? My house or yours?"

"...And if I say I don't like either?"

"If you say that, then we default to barging into your apartment so I can toss you into bed."

"...Your room is fine..."

Apparently, Mahiru didn't want Amane bursting into her bedroom, so she finally relented and agreed to rest in Amane's room instead.

Amane exhaled hard—neither a sigh nor a breath of relief. *I understand why she wouldn't want to let a boy into her room*, he thought as he carried her to his bed. *And I know she didn't make a huge fuss, either. But if she was going to be so stubborn about it, I wish she would have just stayed home and rested up in the first place.*

Mahiru hadn't been in Amane's bedroom since New Year's.

For the moment, he lowered Mahiru onto the bed, then started fishing through his dresser drawers. He figured it would be best if she changed into something she wouldn't have to worry about getting sweat on before going to sleep. He chose the smallest shirt and sweatpants he had, then set them down by Mahiru's side.

"Here. Change into these."

"...But—"

"Or I can strip you."

"I'll get changed..."

Mahiru reluctantly picked up the change of clothes.

Amane was not at all prepared to carry out his threat, and he didn't think Mahiru would have let him anyway. Just thinking about it made him want to die of shame. He was thoroughly relieved to hear that she would play along.

Since he wasn't about to stay and watch her change, Amane quickly left the room and retrieved some sports drinks from his pantry shelf.

After Amane had recovered from his cold the previous year, he had stocked up on prepackaged rice porridge, extra sports drinks, and cooling sheets. His preparations were finally paying off.

Carrying the supplies, along with a towel and some medicine, Amane knocked on the door of his own bedroom and heard a small voice reply, "I've finished changing."

He entered and saw Mahiru looking at him, propped up on his bed, wearing his clothes. As expected, even the smallest clothes he had were too large on Mahiru—*baggy* was probably the most accurate word.

She looked adorable, dressed in clothes that were the wrong size, but Amane drove that thought from his mind and set down the sports drinks and towel on the table beside the bed.

"Will you take some medicine? It's over-the-counter stuff."

"...Sure. I have the same type at home, so I think it's all right."

"Okay."

He went back to the kitchen for a moment and filled a cup with water. While he was there, he fished an ice pack out of the freezer. He recalled the saying "Preparation is the key to success" and smiled to himself about how true that was turning out to be.

Amane hurried back to the bedroom and handed the water to Mahiru, then took some pills out of the packaging and put them in her open palm.

"Take those and drink plenty of water. Then get to sleep."

While Mahiru was swallowing the medicine, he wrapped the ice pack in the towel and set it beside her pillow. As he did, he heard Mahiru mumble "…You're pretty well prepared."

"I'm just doing everything you did for me, you know."

Basically, he was just repeating exactly what Mahiru had done when she nursed him back to health. He was healthy now, so it was only natural that he should return the favor.

"By the way, why were you trying to push yourself so hard?"

"…Because I'm incapable of effective self-management."

"Look, you have to draw the line somewhere. You're always running around, working hard, and your body is probably all worn out. Come to think of it, I guess I owe you an apology for my part in keeping you so busy."

Making his dinner every night had undoubtedly placed an extra burden on Mahiru that she clearly didn't need. She had her own life to deal with, and here she was taking care of him. It was inexcusable, really.

Mahiru's fever seemed to be connected to her fatigue, so Amane wanted to care of her the best he could and let her rest.

"…I've never thought of you as a burden, Amane."

"Really…? Well, even if that's true, think of this as a good opportunity for you to take it easy."

He was happy to hear her say that she didn't find the time they spent together to be taxing, but he still felt guilty about how much attention she had paid to his needs. This was his chance to tend to Mahiru while she got some rest. It would probably actually be better to send her home, but Amane wanted to stay by her side. He knew he would never forgive himself if anything happened to her.

Mahiru hesitated but eventually agreed to lie down.

She buried everything up to her neck under the comforter, then glanced at Amane. She looked slightly embarrassed, probably because she didn't like having someone standing over her while she slept. Amane was about to leave her alone, thinking that he shouldn't stare at girls in their sleep, when he felt something tug at his sleeve. When he looked down, he found Mahiru's small hand grasping at his shirt.

Mahiru was also staring at her hand, caramel-colored eyes wide with shock. She looked just as surprised as he did. A moment passed, and then she quickly released him and buried herself completely under the comforter, pulling it all the way up over her face to hide.

"…Good night," came a feeble mumble from Mahiru, cocooned in the blanket.

Amane scratched his cheek, unsure what to do.

…She gets really anxious when she's not feeling well, huh?

Figuring she would probably forgive him, he turned back the comforter a little bit, until he found Mahiru's hand and grabbed hold of it.

He squeezed it gently, and Mahiru stuck her face out from under the comforter, wearing a troubled expression. But Amane had a feeling that was more from embarrassment than anger.

"…I'm not a child, you know."

"I know. I'll just be here keeping watch so that you won't run away, so don't mind me."

"…I'm not running away this late in the game."

"I wonder. Well, I'll get out of here once you're asleep, so you can relax. Come on, if you want me to leave, hurry up and fall asleep."

Amane was being very direct. But it worked. Mahiru meekly snuggled back down under the comforter, and he felt her squeeze his hand back.

He felt sort of happy, and embarrassed, and for some reason, agitated. It was like someone was tickling the inside of his chest.

Amane kept hold of her slender fingers until he heard her peaceful sleeping breaths.

The following morning, Amane woke up on the sofa and checked the clock as he stretched his stiff body.

It was just past eight in the morning. It wasn't a school day, and he almost never got up this early on the weekends, but Amane wanted to see how Mahiru was doing, so he decided he'd better get a move on. He had peeked in on her just in case during the night and confirmed that she looked like she was sleeping peacefully, but he couldn't tell what her true condition was.

He stood up and stretched, then quietly headed toward his own bedroom and opened the door without making a sound.

He hadn't knocked in case Mahiru was still sleeping, but when he opened the door, she sat up.

Her cheeks were still slightly red, but not as red as the night before, and although her expression was slack and somewhat bleary, her eyes focused when she spotted Amane.

"Morning. How are you feeling? The truth, please."

"…I'm still sluggish."

"Gotcha. I'm going to the convenience store to buy breakfast and something that you might be able to eat."

He did have that rice porridge, but he had the image that sick people ate meal supplement jelly and canned peaches and thought those might be easier to eat, so that's what he was planning to get.

He was relieved to find that she seemed to be doing better than expected, and he pulled another change of clothes out of the dresser and set them on the bed.

"I'm leaving you a change of clothes here. Make sure you take your temperature, too. If you want to wipe off the sweat, go ahead and use the water in that wash basin and this towel."

Before leaving the room, Amane pointed to the basin he had used to wipe the sweat from her face during the night.

Then he retrieved his wallet and left the apartment.

Walking at a leisurely pace, Amane made sure that Mahiru would have plenty of time to wipe herself off and change her clothes, even if her fever slowed her down. The convenience store was located quite close to their apartment building, so he could have made the trip in just a few minutes, but he was careful and took his time shopping.

Amane returned home after spending a solid twenty minutes out of the house and put away the cold items in the refrigerator. When he finally went in to see Mahiru, she had finished changing and was waiting for him.

She also seemed more alert and already looked healthier than the day before. She was smiling faintly.

"Any fever?"

"Thirty-seven point five degrees."

"Hmm, still slightly high… Don't move around too much."

"I kn-know that."

"Do you have an appetite? I've got some rice porridge here, and I also bought pudding and jelly."

He knew he shouldn't let her eat anything too heavy, so he had brought back things that were easy to eat and soft, but what she ate would depend on Mahiru's appetite.

"Oh, sorry you went to the—"

"Don't apologize. You did the same thing for me. So pudding or jelly, which do you want?"

"…Jelly."

"Here ya go. Do you think you can eat some rice porridge as well?"

"…Yes."

"All right, I'll heat it up; so you sit tight."

Amane shuffled out of the room. He was concerned about Mahiru. She seemed anxious. Amane placed a pouch of rice porridge in some hot water to warm it up, then poured it into a bowl.

If he was really going to repay Mahiru for what she did last time, he probably should have made the porridge by hand, but he honestly wasn't sure he would have been able to pull it off without messing up something, so he'd decided to fall back on the reliable instant pouches.

He was sure it would be nothing next to Mahiru's homemade porridge, but Amane figured the most important thing was that she had something, anything, to eat.

"Here. Think you can manage to eat on your own?" Amane asked her jokingly as he held out a spoon and waited for her to take the bowl of porridge.

Mahiru scowled at him sullenly. "Are you making fun of me? And what if I said I can't eat on my own—I suppose you'd offer to feed me?"

"Ah, I mean… I'll feed you if you want, but…"

Mahiru's face went red, as if her fever had made a sudden comeback.

"…I-I'll eat by myself."

"Y-yeah."

She accepted the bowl from Amane and started taking small bites, but the redness did not disappear by the time she was done eating.

She seemed to still have some appetite after finishing the porridge, so she opened the jelly next. Once she put that away as well, she sighed. She looked much better now, so all that was left was to get some rest so she could regain her strength. Amane was rather relieved.

"Is there anything else you want me to do?"

"…Nothing for now."

"All right."

When Amane stood up to leave, thinking that he should probably just let her rest more, Mahiru slowly looked up at him, as if making some sort of request. Her gaze was steady and direct.

Sensing the fear and anxiety lurking behind her caramel-colored eyes, Amane sat down right next to Mahiru.

"...Amane?"

"It's nothing."

If he told her up front that she seemed lonely, Mahiru would probably deny it outright and chase him away.

So Amane sat quietly by the bedside and simply looked over at Mahiru, who was sitting up in bed. "I'm not busy right now anyway. How about we just chat until you get a little sleepy?"

"...Okay." She nodded.

He smiled at her as he leaned against the bed, and Mahiru also smiled faintly as if reassured.

"...This is the first time someone's ever really taken care of me when I'm sick... Even Miss Koyuki went home when her shift was over."

"Miss Koyuki?"

"The maid who worked for us when I was at home."

"Ah, the person who taught you how to cook?"

"...I was always alone in the mornings and evenings, so..."

"Well, I'm here now. Besides, I'll be in a serious pinch if you don't hurry up and get well."

"...I'm sorry for using your bed. And about dinner..."

"That's not what I meant. It's awful, you know? I just want to see my friend get better."

Even though they had only known each other a relatively short while, after all the time they'd spent together, it was only natural for Amane to worry about her. Even if she hadn't been running herself ragged taking care of him among other things, Amane still would have worried about her. She was his friend, after all.

"And besides, I'm not the type of person who celebrates when someone else gets sick."

"...I know that already. You're a nice person, Amane."

"Yes, ma'am."

He was a little embarrassed and felt awkward being told directly to his face that he was nice.

"Go ahead and get some rest... You'll feel better if you sleep as much as you need."

"...Okay."

"Shall I stand guard until you drift off again?"

Amane made a joke to hide his embarrassment, but Mahiru blinked in surprise.

"...Yes, please do."

"Huh?"

"You suggested it."

"I did, but..."

He never imagined that she would accept. He had expected Mahiru to glow bright red and immediately reject the idea. His eyes went wide in surprise, and now Mahiru was the one wearing an impish smile.

"Or does a man go back on his word?"

"...Absolutely not. Time to lie down," Amane muttered quietly. Then he added "You win this round" as he squeezed Mahiru's hand.

She slipped under the covers. Then she looked at her hand resting in Amane's, and her expression softened.

"...It's so warm."

"Your fever must have gone down a lot, if you've cooled off... All right, get some sleep."

"Okay."

She squeezed his hand once in return. She looked like she was relieved that he was there after all. Slowly, her eyes drifted closed, and before long, Amane could hear the regular rhythm of her sleeping breath.

…You dummy, he groaned, covering his face with his other hand.

Whenever the two of them touched like this, Amane lost his cool. His heart was pounding in his ears, and his face felt so hot that, for a moment, he wondered if Mahiru's fever had jumped hosts. Amane was so flushed that he almost forgot which of them was supposed to have the fever.

…This girl is really bad for my heart.

Amane glanced over at Mahiru and saw her sleeping peacefully, entirely relaxed and blissfully ignorant of Amane's woes.

Amane swore under his breath and buried his face in the bedsheets.

It was his bed, but it had a sweet scent, a little different from his own.

When Amane came to, Mahiru's warmth had disappeared.

The hand he had been holding was gone, leaving Amane face-down in the bed, all alone. He looked around the room in alarm, but Mahiru was obviously not in bed.

Amane looked at the clock on the side table, saw that it was two, and then realized that he had crashed. He thought maybe it was because he had gotten up to check on Mahiru during the night, but even so, Amane had never intended to sleep for so long. Flustered, Amane stood up and headed for the living room.

He moved briskly, and it wasn't long before he saw Mahiru sitting with good posture on the living room sofa. She wasn't dressed in his shirt and sweatpants anymore, but in her own clothing, which likely meant that she'd gone home for a bit before returning.

"Amane, good morning."

"Morning. You weren't there when I woke up, so I panicked a little."

"Sorry. I took a quick shower and came back."

That must have been why she had changed clothes. Feeling relieved that she was well enough to bathe, he pressed his palm against Mahiru's forehead just in case, but she was already back to her usual temperature.

"Mm, seems like your fever broke. That's great."

"…I'm sorry for worrying you."

"You should be. Next time I'm going to do the same exact thing if you're not honest with me."

He said this as he was taking a seat next to Mahiru, and she frowned uneasily.

"I'll be careful, but…Amane, won't you be angry if I cause you trouble again?"

"Trouble?"

"Because you had to nurse me and everything…"

"As if I'd ever consider any of that trouble, you dummy. Do I honestly seem that heartless to you?"

"…Not at all. It's just… I was only wondering if it's all right to rely on you."

"You should rely on people for whatever you can. You're definitely the type who tries to take everything upon yourself even when you don't need to."

They had only been together for a few months, but even so, Amane thought he understood Mahiru's temperament pretty well.

She fundamentally didn't like to rely on other people, and she bottled up all her feelings deep inside and tried to never let them show. She seemed like she shut herself off from other people by building a wall that she didn't want anyone to slip behind.

"I mean, I know that I'm not very trustworthy, and you can't rely on me, but—"

"Th-that's not true! I trust you a lot, Amane."

"Good. Then don't force yourself and let me help you."

Without thinking, he reached out and ruffled Mahiru's hair, only after which he noticed that Mahiru had gone completely still.

"Sorry. You hate that, don't you?"

"…Not exactly, no…"

Mahiru shook her head slowly, not to disentangle his hand from her hair, but to disagree with his statement, then leaned her forehead against his upper arm.

His heart leaped in his chest when he felt the slight weight of her body pressing against him, but without revealing it in the least, he patted her head once more. He heard a truly quiet little whisper: "…Thank you so much."

Chapter 6

Valentine's Day

By the beginning of February, rumors concerning Mahiru's "mystery man, possible boyfriend" finally died down, despite the fact that Amane had carelessly added fuel to the fire by picking her up from the station.

Even so, the idea of a boy who was not her boyfriend but was still very close to Mahiru seemed to have taken root instead, and the new rumor was that Mahiru had feelings for that boy...but Mahiru cheerfully denied it all in her friendly but ultimately unyielding way, so eventually the stream of gossip dried up.

Amane had heard from Chitose, who had been observing the situation in the hallways, that "her denial left no room for argument," so it seemed like Mahiru was pretty upset.

He wasn't surprised, but he was a little sad to hear how vehemently she was denying it. Still, he knew there wasn't much to be done about it. The current situation was probably driving Mahiru crazy, having to listen to all these wild rumors about a guy she didn't even like that way.

Amane could do nothing but wear a wry smile.

"So speaking of February...," Chitose prodded.

"Oh yeah, final exams are coming up," Amane said.

"You know, for a teenage boy, you sure lack imagination."

Chitose didn't hide her disapproval at his reply.

She had paid him a visit at his apartment after school—or rather, she had barged in without an invitation—on the pretense that she had something important to discuss, though Amane was pretty sure she'd actually come to hang out with Mahiru.

Incidentally, Mahiru was in the kitchen putting on a pot of tea, so Amane and Chitose were alone in the living room.

"I don't know about other high school guys and their imaginations, but I'd say that's a reasonable train of thought for any student…"

"A high school guy in the prime of his life should be thinking about Valentine's Day, don't you think?"

"I'm not in the prime of anything so no…"

"There you go again!"

Chitose was giving him a mischievous look even though she should know better than most that there was no truth behind the rumors.

Amane glared at her, but her smile refused to crack. "So…," he said with a sigh, "what did you want to talk about?"

Chitose had made a point to come to Amane's apartment alone. She obviously had something she wanted to discuss with Amane and Mahiru, but not with her boyfriend, Itsuki.

"Mm. I wanted to ask you what I should do about chocolates for Itsuki. When we were in middle school, I made him chocolates out of a kit, the kind where you melt the chocolate and pour it into a mold, but since we're high schoolers now, I'd like to make something more sophisticated."

"In that case, Shiina's the one you oughtta ask."

After all, Amane knew nothing about cooking. At most, he might be able to offer some insight into his best friend's tastes, but Chitose had actually been dating Itsuki for longer than Amane had known him, so she probably knew what Itsuki liked better than he did.

"I'm gonna ask her, too, but I thought since you're sorta a guy... you know? Maybe I could get a male opinion."

"I'm not sorta anything. I'm all man."

"If you were a real man, you'd have made a move on a certain pretty girl by now," Chitose said slyly.

"Now, listen," Amane said with a grimace, "I've explained this before—we don't have that sort of relationship. And besides, a real man is supposed to wait until he's in a relationship to make a move."

"Oh, how wonderfully chivalrous of you," Chitose teased. "Your mama must have raised you right."

Chitose might think he was uptight, but Amane didn't see anything wrong with wanting to take it slow. Sure, plenty of guys could mess around with girls they didn't even like, but *could* wasn't the same as *should*. More importantly, Amane couldn't see himself doing that, especially if the other party just wasn't interested.

Now, it would have been a lie to say that he didn't have certain feelings for Mahiru. Spending time with a girl so beautiful—inside and out—would stir up those sorts of emotions in most any man.

But even then, the foolish idea to try something with had her never surfaced.

Whenever he thought about it, all kinds of other things got in the way—worrying about hurting her feelings, worrying that she might come to hate him, worrying that he did not appreciate her enough.

Also, Mahiru had made it quite clear that trying anything would result in serious social repercussions, as well as grievous physical harm to a certain vital organ, and he did not think that she was bluffing.

"Well, that's one of your good points, Amane, and I'm sure it's why Mahirun feels like she can trust you."

Chitose had started referring to Mahiru by a nickname that had a cute ring to it.

Mahiru was listening in from the kitchen, but she didn't stop Chitose from calling her that, so whether she was reluctant or comfortable with the name herself, she must have known that she had a nickname now.

As far as Mahiru was concerned, it was better than being called an angel to her face.

"Though sometimes I wonder whether you're really a man at all…," Chitose continued.

"I can assure you, I am. I mean, have you ever seen a girl this flat?"

"Well, you're much too passive. A man is supposed to be a little ferocious sometimes."

"You think a guy like me could pull off *ferocious?*"

"You'd be fine if you dressed the part like those other times. Honestly, I'd like to see it for myself."

Itsuki and Chitose had long since deduced that Amane was Mahiru's mystery man, and he had finally acknowledged it just the other day, so there was no point in hiding it now. But he wasn't about to get all dressed up just for their amusement.

"Give it up already."

"Come on; it's no big deeeal!"

"I can't spare the hair wax—or the patience, for that matter."

"Cheapskate!"

When Mahiru returned from the kitchen carrying a tray with three cups of milk tea, Chitose had puffed out her cheeks and was pouting at him. Mahiru smiled as she set the tray on the coffee table.

Amane sprung up from the sofa and moved to a cushion on the floor, gesturing for Mahiru to sit down. She gingerly took the now-vacant seat, looking apologetic.

"But if you look good enough to gossip about," Chitose continued, "imagine how popular you'd be if you dressed that way all the time."

"No way. It's a huge hassle, and I don't even wanna be popular in the first place."

"Whaaat? Not even with Valentine's Day coming up? Don't you want to get lots of chocolate, Amane? Like, he's just one example, but Yuu's super popular, and it seems like he gets tons of chocolates. Aren't you the slightest bit jealous?"

"No way. I'd get diabetes."

By Yuu, Chitose must have been referring to Yuuta. Assigning weird nicknames to people seemed to be one of Chitose's many habits. Fortunately, she hadn't gotten around to thinking of one for Amane.

Maybe Yuuta—dubbed the prince—did receive tons of chocolate, but there was no way he could eat it all without getting fat.

"Anyway, it's depressing just to think about the returns," Amane added. "I mean, between the chocolates people just give out to be polite and the ones people give out to confess their feelings, Kadowaki's probably on the receiving end of several dozen gifts, and then he has to pay all those back threefold. That's gotta be hell on a high school student's wallet."

"How admirable to assume that he's going to pay everything back threefold. Well, I'm going to give you some chocolate, and you don't need to worry about return gifts or anything like that. What kind do you like?"

"I'm not really into sweet things, so...something not too sweet."

"Got it; I'll come up with something."

"Don't put anything funny in there."

"It's fine; it'll all be edible."

"Hey..."

Amane wasn't sure what Chitose was planning, but he was

definitely expecting something more than an ordinary box of chocolates.

"Mahirun, who are you giving chocolate to?"

"The girls I'm friends with in my class."

"Not to any boys?"

"…If I give anyone chocolate, even courtesy chocolate, they take it the wrong way, so…"

"Ah-ha."

Amane could easily imagine the uproar among the boys—and the pointless fighting that was sure to follow. Most of the boys in his class would treat chocolate from the school angel like mana from heaven, so if word got around that Mahiru was giving out chocolate, it would definitely mean trouble. Amane wasn't sure whether Mahiru's popularity or the boys' foolishness was more to blame.

Obviously, it's safer for Mahiru to avoid giving out any chocolate at all.

Amane nodded and smiled to himself.

"Oh, and I'll also save some chocolate for you, Chitose."

"Yaaay! I love you, Mahirun. I'll give you some, too. The real stuff, not like what I'm giving Amane."

"I heard that!"

Chitose was grinning widely as she squeezed Mahiru tight.

Amane was relieved to see the way she was touching Mahiru didn't constitute sexual harassment, but he kept a sharp eye on Chitose to make it clear he wouldn't let her get away with anything.

"I'm just joookiiing. I'm gonna give you the edible stuff, too, okay, Amane?"

"I have a feeling that edible and tasty are two very different things here…"

Amane pressed a hand to his forehead. He could feel a headache coming on. Chitose was certainly excited about her latest plot. She didn't even try to hide her delight as she laughed at Amane.

"I'm sure you'll enjoy your present!"

On Valentine's Day, as Amane had predicted, the mood at school was tense. Everyone was restless; no one could settle down. Many people believed that a guys' social status depended on whether he received chocolates on Valentine's Day. At the moment, most of the boys were trying to act like they weren't desperately waiting for something.

"Everyone's all worked up, huh?"

It certainly seemed nerve-racking. Amane, on the other hand, didn't care a bit about his social standing, so he had the privilege of watching the day pass through the eyes of a remote observer. His attention turned to Itsuki, who also had nothing to worry about today, though for a different reason.

"Looks that way," Itsuki answered, staring nonchalantly across the classroom.

"Mr. Itsuki, as a man with a girlfriend—a man who, I might add, appears totally calm today—we'd like to ask for your opinion on this year's Valentine's Day proceedings."

"Well, Amane, the boys certainly look desperate. Understandable, considering that whether they receive chocolates today can have major ramifications on their sense of pride as men in the coming weeks. And let's not forget that approximately sixty percent of these fine young fellows are, at this very moment, sweating over whether they might receive chocolates from the lovely lady Shiina."

"...Apparently, she's not giving anything to the guys, not even courtesy chocolate. Since it would get out of hand."

"Yeah, I guess it would... By the way, do you think you're getting anything from a certain someone?"

"No idea. At least, I haven't seen any indication that I might."

Mahiru was giving chocolates to the girls but not the guys, so Amane didn't expect that she was going to give him any. Of course, he would feel grateful if she did give him some, but he was fine either way.

Honestly, as far as Amane was concerned, Valentine's Day was all just a big sales promotion cooked up by confectionery companies, so it wasn't something he really cared about.

Itsuki chuckled at his friend's obvious disinterest. "You sure are blunt, Amane." Then his attention turned to a particularly lively corner of the classroom. "Now, that... That's somethin', all right."

Itsuki was gesturing toward a handsome young man with a captivating smile surrounded by a group of girls all jostling to hand him different bags and boxes of chocolates.

Class hadn't even started yet, and already the bag that the boy had apparently brought expressly as a receptacle was stuffed full of presents, undeniable proof of his tremendous popularity.

"I don't know whether to say 'It figures' or what."

"You can just feel the hatred wafting off the other guys."

The boys shooting Yuuta envious looks or staring hopelessly into the distance likely had not received anything from anyone yet. The difference between their social standings was obvious.

It must be a real pain to have to carry home so much chocolate, Amane told himself, wondering what he would even do with that much candy.

"Popular guys have it rough, huh? What do you think he even does with it all?"

"Yeah, seriously. I'm amazed he doesn't get fat. It's been like this ever since middle school, but his figure hasn't changed at all."

"You can definitely tell he's a track-and-field guy. Well, at least that's a problem I won't have to worry about."

"Not so fast. Chitose really outdid herself this time. You'd better prepare yourself."

"Whaddaya mean 'prepare myself'?"

"It's a Russian roulette."

"Knock it off. What'd she mix in?"

Their exchange the previous day heavily implied that Chitose wasn't planning to make normal sweets, but Itsuki made it sound like she'd used some incredibly questionable ingredients.

"Let's see, one piece is a three-in-one habanero, wasabi, and hot pepper chocolate. Another has pickled plum concentrate jelly in it. And the rest are normal chocolate."

"What the hell has she created?"

"Apparently, she wanted to surprise you, Amane."

In a certain sense, he was surprised, but it was mostly in the *about to faint* sense.

"...Now I'm afraid to eat them."

"Surrender all hope. I've already walked this thorny path."

"I bet you ate them all for a laugh."

"Maybe. As long as Chi makes it, I'll eat anything."

"You two sicken me."

Itsuki might put whatever Chitose offered him into his mouth without a second thought, but Amane wasn't so trusting.

Chitose wasn't actually all that bad at cooking; the problem was that she always got carried away with her next grand idea. She was perfectly capable of preparing entirely ordinary dishes; she just chose to create culinary calamities sometimes.

While her main victim was Itsuki, Amane was surprised to suddenly find himself in the crosshairs. That said, from the way Itsuki was acting, he didn't think it could be too terrible. There was probably nothing to worry about, despite the agonized faces that Itsuki was making.

Still, Amane couldn't help but shake a strange feeling of melancholy.

"Okay, Amane, here you go!" Chitose said, handing him his chocolates. She had caught up with Amane and Itsuki in their classroom after school.

"...Thank you," Amane replied somewhat reluctantly.

He didn't want to seem ungrateful, though he had to admit he was a little concerned about the chocolates she had made. He was still going to eat them all, obviously, but he wasn't looking forward to finding the super-spicy and super-sour chocolates she'd apparently hidden in the batch.

"I'm sure you've heard from Itsuki, but be ready for something exciting!"

"I don't really like spicy food..."

"It's not that bad, you wuss! I taste tested everything myself. In fact, I thought the hot one was actually really good!"

"Yeah, but you *like* spicy stuff...," Amane moaned. "Geez..."

Amane didn't like spicy or sour food. It was like Chitose had gone out of her way to include flavors that Amane couldn't handle. On the other hand, the rest of the chocolates were sure to be really delicious, so...

"Oh, and there's also a super-sweet one and a super-bitter one mixed in."

"Thanks for the warning...," Amane groaned. It was just like Chitose to add in a few extra land mines at the last minute.

The super-sweet one probably featured condensed milk, while the super-bitter one was probably made of close to 99 percent cacao chocolate. That actually didn't sound too bad. Amane handled bitter foods better than most.

Saekisan * 119

Apparently, this was the first time Itsuki was hearing this, and his face twitched as he murmured, "Chi...you're unbelievable..."

Chitose continued smiling. "It'll be fine. There's even a special palate cleanser in there."

"And what might that be?" Amane asked.

"All right, we're going now, bye-byeee." Without answering Amane's question, Chitose grabbed Itsuki's hand and walked off. Apparently, they had a Valentine's date to get to.

"Good luck, man!" Itsuki offered as he was pulled away.

Amane let out an exhausted sigh and waved good-bye. After watching them disappear from sight, he pulled on his coat, thinking it was about time for him to head home, too, and picked up his bag from the hook on the side of his desk.

Amane usually didn't mind being alone, but today he felt out of place among all the lovesick boys and girls. He shouldered his bag and glanced around the room.

The flurry of gift giving seemed to have finally subsided. Yuuta sat staring vacantly at the enormous pile of presents on his desk. The other boys in the class could only dream of such a hoard, and the bag hanging from the side of his desk was stuffed full of even more treasures.

Amane could guess what was weighing on Yuuta's mind and couldn't help but feel bad for him. He approached the other boy's desk.

"Kadowaki?"

"Hmm? Ah, Fujimiya. What's up?"

They had been classmates for almost a year, so he remembered Amane's name, even though Amane didn't have much of a presence in class.

He had never taken the initiative to talk to Yuuta before, outside of a few group assignments, and the other boy seemed curious about the sudden interaction.

Amane responded to his confusion with an awkward smile, then undid the zipper of a small pocket on the front of his bag.

"Nothing in particular, just, here—"

From the pocket, Amane pulled out several plastic supermarket bags, folded into compact triangles, and tossed them to Yuuta.

Mahiru had put them there and told him, "Keep a few of these in your bag. That way you'll have them whenever you need them." He had imagined he might use them for garbage or maybe in case of motion sickness, but he'd never expected them to come in handy like this.

Looking perplexed by the strange bundles, Yuuta unfolded one of the triangles to reveal a relatively large disposable shopping bag. The plastic didn't look particularly durable, but Amane decided that Yuuta would just have to manage somehow.

"Did I…uh…read the situation wrong?" Amane asked.

"N-no…," Yuuta replied. "You're right on target, but—"

"Great. Well, good luck with all that." Reflecting on the many hazards of popularity, Amane waved good-bye and left the classroom.

Later, Yuuta was spotted around the school carrying several shopping bags stuffed to bursting.

Though it was Valentine's Day, that didn't mean that there was anything special in the air at home, and Amane went back to his apartment to relax just like always.

It was too early to start making dinner, so he and Mahiru lounged beside each other on the couch. She didn't seem excited or on edge in any way, and Amane took this as a sign that she was definitely not planning anything special today.

He didn't mind, since he wasn't expecting anything in the first place, but couldn't quite dispel the slight disappointment that he chalked up to his manly pride.

"There was a sweet smell hanging over the school today, huh?" Amane remarked.

"It is Valentine's Day," Mahiru replied.

Amane had heard a lot of disappointed grumbling coming from the boys in his class. Mahiru had only given chocolates to her female friends—she hadn't even handed out courtesy chocolates to the boys.

Amane wondered why any of them had assumed they might receive anything in the first place—it wasn't like they had any kind of relationship with her…but nevertheless, they had high hopes.

"Well, Valentine's Day really only matters to the popular guys anyway. It's got nothing to do with lackluster guys like me…"

"How very perceptive of you," Mahiru remarked.

"I'm not exactly proud to say this," Amane continued unprompted, "but I've never received a romantic gift from anyone. Though, I did just get some Russian roulette courtesy chocolates from Chitose."

"Russian roulette courtesy chocolates?"

"Apparently, mixed in among the normal chocolates are some… exciting concoctions."

It was impossible to tell the super-spicy, super-sour, super-sweet, and super-bitter chocolates from the rest, and any one of them seemed capable of obliterating his sense of taste. Amane was kind of afraid to start eating at all.

"Another amazing creation…"

"Well, I'll eat them later, but please show some sympathy if you find me rolling around in agony."

"You're going to eat them all?"

"The thing is… She sorta made them just for me, so I kinda feel obligated to eat them. Besides, it's not like they're poisonous or anything."

The chocolates might be extra stimulating, but it wasn't like they would cause him any real harm, and Chitose had gone out of her way to make and deliver them, so he was one hundred percent planning to eat them all with gratitude in his heart. Still, the exciting ingredients made him rather nervous.

"...Is that how it is?" Mahiru muttered.

"Well, it's not like I got any other chocolates, and for a loner like me, Valentine's Day doesn't mean much besides an excuse to eat some candy."

Amane was perfectly content with a single courtesy gift. He was already worried about the day one month from now when he would have to repay Chitose's present and wondered what he should get her.

Mahiru simply stared at him silently.

After dinner, Amane decided to sample one of Chitose's chocolates and ended up facedown on his desk in agony.

Chitose had arranged evenly spaced partitions containing twelve truffles inside the box. There were four varieties of "surprise" chocolate. That meant he had a one-in-three chance of picking something that would give his taste buds the shock of a lifetime. Among those, the worst was sure to be the super-spicy one. Amane figured that he could handle the rest without too much trouble, but—

"You found one, didn't you?" Mahiru asked in a sympathetic tone. She had been in the kitchen preparing drinks and returned to find Amane in obvious distress.

"...I was planning to eat them all over a few days, and this is what I get..."

Amane quickly quaffed his drink, but the inside of his mouth was beyond hot. This went beyond having a low tolerance for spicy food—he was in real pain here. It wasn't more than he could handle, but it was still pretty intense.

As the characteristically sharp sting of wasabi shot through his nose, Amane found himself thinking how impressive it was that Chitose had managed to include so much of the volatile component. He cursed her name while trying to hold back the instinctive tears.

The wasabi attacked his nose and eyes, while the habanero powder and hot pepper burned his tongue. A single nibble of these intense flavors—or rather, intense torments—was enough to ruin him.

"My condolences," Mahiru said. "But think of it this way—if you make it through hell first, the rest will be heaven."

Easy for her to say. Amane was still in agony. He heard a soft sigh and then the sound of something hard being set down beside him.

"Here, this should help."

When he raised his head, there was a mug beside him, filled with a dark-brown liquid, giving off steam and a sweet aroma.

"Cocoa?"

"Something like that. It's called *chocolat chaud*. It's French hot chocolate. I made it fairly sweet. It should help cleanse your palate."

"I'm saved…"

Right now, the only thing Amane wanted to do was to wash away this pain.

As Amane tipped the contents of the mug into his mouth, a rich flavor enveloped his senses. The liquid had the luscious fragrance of full-bodied chocolate but was actually not that sweet. It tasted like dark chocolate and possessed a calming flavor that went down very easily.

"It's great."

"I'm glad to hear it."

Amane slowly sipped the hot chocolate, attempting to soothe the pain in his mouth. The truffle hadn't actually contained very much of the spicy mixture. It had mostly been ganache coated in a thick layer of chocolate and covered in powdered sugar. The weaponized sweet packed a big kick up front, but the impact faded as time went on. By the time Amane had drained his mug, he was left with only a slight tingle on his tongue.

"*Sigh...* She really outdid herself..."

"Was it really that spicy?"

"I mean, it had pepper and wasabi and habanero in it, so yeah. Damn... I'm glad you made that palate cleanser, but I think I would've died if I ate any more."

"Well, I suppose there's no harm done."

"Good grief."

Even as he cursed Chitose's name under his breath, he knew that she had tried in her own way to surprise him, so he couldn't really be upset with her. All the chocolates besides the special four probably tasted normal, so it wasn't like there was any malice behind it. And she had even tried all the exotic ingredients herself. Amane could do nothing but smile bitterly.

"Anyway, the hot chocolate was a nice surprise. Usually you stick to hot milk, right?"

"...Yes, well..."

"Did you decide to make this because it's Valentine's Day?" Amane asked hopefully. Mahiru basically always drank hot milk or milk tea, so the cocoa was unexpected.

"...Maybe."

"Well, thank you. You're a lifesaver."

Mahiru responded with a small nod, and Amane breathed a quiet sigh of relief.

He had gone out on a limb there, and if she had shot him down, he would have looked like a real idiot. But apparently, he'd been right on the money. Mahiru had wanted to do something special for Valentine's Day after all. Amane was sure there wasn't any deeper meaning to it than that, but he was still grateful.

"It was delicious," he said again.

Mahiru seemed uncomfortable.

"Is something the matter?" he prodded.

"…Um, well—"

"Hmm?"

Amane knew that sitting beside her and pressing her for an answer would probably just make it harder for her to tell him, so he tried to be patient and listen instead.

Mahiru hugged one of the pillows over half her face as she stared up at him anxiously. She looked like a small and strangely adorable animal, which made Amane want to smile and reach out and pat her on the head. He continued waiting, but instead of continuing her thought, Mahiru simply trembled silently.

Then she stood up suddenly and grabbed her bags.

"…I'm…going home."

By the time Amane let out a noise of surprise, Mahiru had already slipped out of the living room. He was frozen in place as he listened to the sound of her receding footsteps, then the front door opening and closing, and finally the sound of the lock turning. In a flash, Mahiru was gone.

He couldn't help letting out a confused noise at this quick work. "Eh…?"

Did I do something wrong…?

His heart was torn between surprise at her unexpected departure and worry that he had inadvertently driven her away. He stood up, thinking about what he should do if Mahiru was still in a bad mood when he saw her tomorrow, and went to check the front door. Suddenly, he caught sight of a light-pink paper bag hanging from the doorknob of his room. Mahiru must have left it there.

Inside the bag was a pastel-pink box tied with a chocolate-colored ribbon, and there was a card affixed to the front with a sticker. The handwriting was smooth and neat.

Thank you for always being there for me. Please accept this with my gratitude.

Amane realized why she had left the bag there. Just handing it to him would have been too awkward, especially after she had decided not to give chocolate to any other boys.

She could have just given it to me...

Smiling gently at how surprisingly timid Mahiru could be in these sorts of situations, Amane sat back down on the sofa and examined the contents of the bag.

The adorable wrapping paper reminded him of Mahiru's sophisticated yet feminine style.

Amane figured it was all right for him to go ahead and open it, and with some apprehension, he slowly unwrapped the box.

Inside were candied orange rings dipped in chocolate, each individually wrapped in plastic—in other words, orangettes.

The contrast between the bright color and the deep luster of the chocolate was dazzling to the eye, and the box even included a few with white chocolate coating, and some used lemon peels instead of oranges. They looked delicious, and Amane appreciated the variety.

There was a second card accompanying the Orangettes.

You don't seem to like sweet things too much, so I made you something that I thought would better suit your tastes. I hope you like it.

He recalled a conversation from about ten days earlier.

"What kind do you like?"

"I'm not really into sweet things, so...something not too sweet."

Apparently, Mahiru had remembered his conversation with Chitose perfectly and picked something that would match his tastes. Amane suddenly felt very self-conscious. He hadn't expected to receive anything at all, and here she had selected something especially for him. It was typical of the sensitive, considerate Mahiru. Amane could feel himself starting to blush just thinking about it.

He reached down and picked up one of the orangettes, appreciating the beautiful colors as he unwrapped the candy and slowly took a bite. The sugary and astringent bite of the candied orange peel melded perfectly with the pleasantly bitter chocolate in his mouth, each flavor complimenting the other in a splendid harmony.

...So good...

Amane marveled at how Mahiru's handmade confections were much better than anything he'd ever gotten from the store as he took another bite.

Mahiru's orangettes were a little sour, a little bitter—and intensely sweet.

"Hey, Fujimiya, thanks for yesterday."

The following morning, Yuuta casually approached Amane at school. He seemed cheerful and friendly, but Amane couldn't help but feel nervous talking to him. Even though they had briefly spoken the day before, Amane never would have expected him to go out of his way to come say thanks just for that.

A few people shot them curious glances, which only made Amane even more nervous. He didn't like being the center of attention.

"Oh, don't worry about it. You looked like you were having a hard time."

"Well, yeah..." Yuuta got a faraway look in his eyes

"I bet being a popular guy is really tough, huh?" Amane tried to sympathize.

Yuuta was clearly aware of his popularity, but it wasn't the kind of thing he would ever flaunt. That was part of why everybody liked him—and why even the most jealous boys couldn't bring themselves to truly hate him. He was the kind of guy who would come over and thank you for something as trivial as a plastic bag.

"Anyway, it was a big help. Just wanted to say thanks."

"Don't mention it. Glad I could help a guy in need."

He hadn't offered to help so that Yuuta would owe him or anything. Amane smiled to show that he thought it was no big deal, and Yuuta smiled back, looking relieved. The girls in the class all squealed. Amane couldn't help but laugh bitterly as he wished that Yuuta would save his smile for his admirers.

"What did you do for Yuuta?" Itsuki asked after Yuuta left. Apparently, he had been watching the exchange.

"Kadowaki had too much chocolate, so I gave him a couple plastic bags."

"Ah. So he ended up with more than he expected. Shoulda come prepared." Itsuki smiled sympathetically.

The two of them had watched Yuuta pile up the presents and agreed that he would probably have a hard time making it home with the whole score. Itsuki wasn't surprised that Amane had decided to help out.

As far as Amane was concerned, it was really just a small gesture. Nothing worth going out of your way to say thank you for.

"Well, that's all it was. Nothing too important."

"That's just like you, man... But wait, you're keeping a bunch of old plastic bags around? Aren't you getting a little too engrossed in the domestic life? When I saw you scanning grocery store ads on your phone, I thought you were somebody's housewife."

"Hey, whose wife is that supposed to be? Last time I checked, I was still a man. Though, I'll admit that maybe I've been heavily influenced by you-know-who..."

Without a doubt, he could say it was all Mahiru's fault. The two of them were splitting food expenses, so he had been checking online ads, thinking he had better get the best deals he could, then suggesting things they could make from whatever was on sale. Apparently, that reminded Itsuki more of a housewife than a husband. Though he did leave the cooking entirely up to Mahiru.

"Must be nice to have a partner to play house."

"She's not really my partner. And what about Chitose?"

"Chi? Well, sure. So long as I can keep her from getting carried away with her weird experiments anyway. I mean, she knows how to cook, for sure."

"...Does she ever make anything that's *not* weird?"

"That's just part of her charm, all right?" Itsuki's eyes darted from side to side.

"Whatever you need to tell yourself, man."

For better or worse, there was rarely a dull moment with Chitose. She might've looked like an ordinary high school girl, and apparently she even had some surprising talents on the home front, but when the mood struck her, she was liable to cause all sorts of trouble.

"Well, it sounds like she's going to get it together after we're married, so—"

"How long do you think it's going to take to get your dad to accept her...?"

Itsuki's father, who was oddly strict about dating in a way that you didn't see much these days, had never approved of Chitose. He would definitely have something to say if he heard that they were planning to get married.

Chitose's parents, on the other hand, were apparently ready to welcome Itsuki into the family at any time, which always confused Amane... Wasn't it usually the other way around?

"Well, once we're adults, he'll have to come around. I'll threaten him with not seeing his grandkids and all that. This is one fight where I can't back down and just do what my dad wants."

Itsuki made a show of shrugging like he didn't think much of it, but Amane noticed the serious look in his eyes. He was obviously not planning to budge on this issue.

Amane had always understood the extent to which Itsuki loved Chitose, so he chose to encourage them, admiring how amazing it was that they were thinking about marriage even while they were still in high school.

"...Well, I think you're probably not one to back down until you've got a ring on her finger, so I wish you the best of luck."

"Yeah. And good luck to you, too," Itsuki replied.

"At what?"

"I mean, with you-know-who... Right?"

"...I don't really have that kind of relationship with her. Don't make things up."

Amane turned away sharply, but he could hear Itsuki's bright, cheerful laughter.

Amane purchased everything he needed at the supermarket and headed home. When he got there, Mahiru was already in his apartment, sitting on the sofa, waiting in her usual spot. She had her knees pulled up and was squeezing a cushion to her chest. The position made her look a little childish, but her expression wasn't sulky or dour. Rather, she looked embarrassed.

Well, thank goodness she's wearing a long skirt, Amane thought as he carefully averted his eyes and went to put the dinner ingredients away in the refrigerator. When he returned to the living room, Mahiru was still sitting there waiting for him.

When Amane sat down next to her, Mahiru carefully averted her eyes.

"Mahiru, thank you for the gift yesterday. It was really delicious."

"...I'm glad to hear it."

Amane thought that if she was nervous about what happened yesterday, the best thing to do was to show her how much he appreciated it. Mahiru continued squeezing the cushion but didn't say anything else.

"What would you like in return?" Amane asked.

"That's not why I gave it to you..."

"I know that, but well, give a favor, get a favor, right? It wouldn't be very gentlemanly of me if all I do is take, take, take."

Amane believed that a man should always strive to pay back whatever he received. Since Mahiru had gone out of her way to make him such delicious treats, he intended to give her something equally splendid in return. She hadn't made chocolates for any other boy, after all, yet she had made something special that she knew he would like. It must have been a lot of work, all for his sake.

"...I already get so many things from you, Amane."

"Actually, I'm pretty sure I'm the one who's been on the receiving end. You're always cooking for me and stuff. I always feel like I'm just taking advantage of you."

"I do those things because I like doing them. Amane, you probably don't even realize how much you've done for me. But as far as I'm concerned, I've already received more than enough, so I don't need anything else."

Amane genuinely could not imagine what he might have offered Mahiru. It seemed like she was always doing things for him, and he wanted to pay her back for all her kindness...but the tally was apparently very different from Mahiru's perspective.

"Well, that is that, and this is this. I'll try to think of something you might like."

No matter what Amane might have done for her until now, he still wanted to get her a White Day present. It was tradition to repay any Valentine's Day chocolates on White Day, after all.

Amane stared firmly at Mahiru, indicating that he had no intention of giving in on this, until she nodded, her eyes wandering around the room a bit.

"...Fine."

"All right, so I've got about a month to figure out what to give you. It would be great if I could find something that you would really like."

"...Do you have time for a search like that?" Mahiru asked, sounding slightly exasperated. "Next week we have final exams, and then right after, there's the closing ceremony."

Sure enough, finals were only days away.

There had still been a lingering aftertaste of Valentine's Day at school that day, but soon it would be replaced with the typical prickly energy of pre-exam anxiety.

Amane wasn't particularly nervous about it, though.

"If the exams go the same as usual," he said, "I'm sure I'll pass, so I'm not going to stress about them now. Same for you, I bet."

"That's true," Mahiru replied. "I make a point to get my work done with time to spare."

Amane was always diligent when it came to keeping up with his classwork, so he rarely had any trouble with tests. He knew he could maintain his usual grades without any last-minute cram sessions. At most, he might spend a little extra time reviewing the material right before each test.

Mahiru had actually already completed all the coursework in advance, and she was just as diligent about studying as Amane was, so he had never seen her panic about schoolwork. Instead, exam days with their shortened schedules were probably like half days for her.

"Well, don't expect too much."

"...Okay. I'll treasure anything you give me."

"Hey, don't get carried away now."

"I've been taking very good care of Mr. Bear."

"I'm glad to hear it." Amane smiled.

Apparently, Mahiru really treasured the stuffed bear he had given her on her birthday. He had also seen her using the key holder, and she seemed to be taking good care of that as well. He had worried a little bit about how the stuffed bear was faring, but…from all indications, Mahiru really liked it.

Amane could feel his mouth curling up into a grin when he heard Mahiru cutely refer to Mr. Bear, but he thought she might scowl at him if she caught him smiling, so he put on his best poker face.

If we're still hanging out when her next birthday rolls around, what sort of thing can I give her…? he wondered anxiously.

Suddenly, Amane noticed that Mahiru was staring at him.

"…Come to think of it, I don't know when your birthday is," she said.

"Uh, mine? Mine is November eighth."

Guess I never told her, huh?

When she heard his birthday, Mahiru's eyes narrowed…ever so slightly. They had been spending a lot of time together for several months, so he had come to understand that expression as the one she made when she was angry or annoyed.

"…Hey, Amane?"

"Hmm?"

"Didn't we already know each other by then?"

"Yeah, I guess so."

"Why didn't you say anything?"

"Because you never asked. You didn't tell me your birthday, either, remember? I only knew because I saw it on your school ID."

"Urk—"

"And we weren't that close back then anyway. If I had told you my birthday, you would have wondered why in the world I was bringing it up."

Also, Amane hadn't wanted to come across like he was fishing for a present or anything. That would not have been a good look. So he hadn't seen the need to tell her about his birthday—they hadn't had that kind of relationship back then.

"...But—"

"You really don't have to worry about it," Amane insisted.

"Fine...," Mahiru said. "But we'll definitely celebrate your birthday properly this year." As she said that, she turned to him and grasped his sleeve tightly.

Mahiru obviously didn't want this unequal situation to continue. He had never seen someone so serious about a birthday before.

Amane couldn't help but grin—not his normal, wry smirk, but an honest, happy smile.

After all, nothing could make him happier than hearing that Mahiru felt the same way he did...and that she was thinking about spending time together in the future.

"So you're planning to stay with me at least that long, are you?" he prodded.

Mahiru's bright, caramel-colored eyes went wide—and then, in an instant, her face flushed red, and where she had been gripping his sleeve a moment ago, she whacked him with the cushion, obviously trying to hide her embarrassment. Amane could feel himself smiling again at how charming she was.

"...Well, I suppose I don't hate the thought... I always feel so calm when we're together. It's nice."

"Oh really? Thanks."

"But you know I don't really...have any other intentions."

"I knew that already." Amane nodded. "And that's fine with me."

For some reason, Mahiru looked slightly disappointed.

©Hanekoto

©Hanekoto

Chapter 7

White Day

Amane was always diligent with his studies and serious about his lessons, so he completed his final exams without any particular difficulty.

Going over his tests with Mahiru, he found that he'd gotten the same grades as usual. He always did well enough at school and never had to worry about being held back a grade or anything like that.

Itsuki also got fairly good scores, and even Chitose had apparently done well enough to avoid a failing mark, so the people Amane was closest to were in no danger of repeating a year, either.

All that was left was the graduation ceremony to send off the third-year students, which didn't have much to do with them, and after that, to wait for the closing ceremony. Between the two ceremonies, however, was one very important date.

"…What do I give her?"

The day was fast approaching for all those who had prevailed on Valentine's Day to repay their gifts. Both Mahiru and Chitose had given Amane chocolates, so naturally he was planning to give them each something in return. The only problem was that he had no idea what to give Mahiru.

Chitose's gift was easy enough—he planned to combine a White

Day cake from the store where she had purchased their Christmas cake with a sundry of merchandise based on the characters she liked.

He was sure that someone like Chitose, who was more interested in sweets than sweethearts, would appreciate that. It was an obvious choice.

But Mahiru remained a dilemma.

Amane was sure that Mahiru would graciously accept anything he got her—the thought mattered more to her than the actual gift. But he wanted to pick out something that would make her really happy. The trouble was that he honestly didn't know much about the kinds of things she liked. He knew she had a taste for sweets and liked cute stuff like most other girls, but beyond that, he was lost. Mahiru was not an easy person to shop for.

Amane remembered her telling him that she wanted a new whet-stone, but that didn't seem like a particularly charming gift, and he couldn't really afford something like that anyway. And for this occasion, it seemed more appropriate to give her something she would enjoy, rather than something practical.

Amane started his search by looking over the White Day display at a nearby department store, but he couldn't picture Mahiru being truly happy with any of the things there. Amane was hoping for a reaction like he'd gotten when he'd given her the stuffed bear.

Of course, it would be boring to give her a stuffed animal a second time.

There were many adorable stuffed animals on display, but Amane decided that a repeat gift lacked originality.

On the other hand, when he tried to imagine what would impress her, Amane's poor imagination could only come up with cosmetics or fashion accessories.

But he knew less than nothing about cosmetics, and he wasn't sure whether they had the kind of relationship where he could confidently

pick out fashionable things for her. He didn't think she would inter-
pret it as anything strange, but he wasn't sure it would really impress
her, either.

Amane thought that their relationship was pretty good, and if he
were Itsuki and she were Chitose, an accessory would be an obvious
choice, but Amane just didn't think it was the right move here.

Racked with worry, Amane lingered restlessly by the gifts corner.
He imagined that he must look awfully suspicious. Even though he
had taken the precaution of dressing up to go out, he thought that a
single guy hanging around the cute goods had to seem shady.

He was grumbling to himself about his options, when from behind
him a voice asked, "Are you looking for anything in particular?"

When Amane turned around, there was a young woman in a
store apron standing there smiling. She had probably noticed his distress as he helplessly wandered the aisles.

"Ah, um... I'm not sure what to get for a White Day present."

"So nothing in the display jumps out at you? Well, there are some
things in our regular stock that are also popular White Day gifts. Let
me show you."

"Ah, no, that's not exactly it... You see, our relationship is rather
hard to define, and I'm not sure what I can get her that won't be...
too much."

"Meaning what?"

"Well, she's not my girlfriend, but we are pretty close, so...this is
just an example, but I'm wondering whether she would be happy to
get an accessory or something from a guy she doesn't like...that way."

As Amane explained his predicament, the store clerk let a little
giggle slip out. She seemed to find his dilemma quite charming.

"I've seen a lot of gentlemen come through here with the same
sort of worries."

"So what did they end up doing?"

"They were all worried, too, but most of them decided to buy something. If you're close to this girl, she'll probably appreciate anything you give her."

Amane felt relieved to hear someone else say that, though of course the prospect of picking an accessory for Mahiru was still fairly daunting.

She was very particular about her attire, and the bits and pieces he had seen her wearing before had all been quite elegant. Amane had no confidence that he could select something that would meet the standards of such a sophisticated young woman.

"Sir, would you like me to show you some of the items in the corner over there that are popular with our female customers?"

"...Yes, please," Amane said gratefully, straightening up a little.

"And so you bought something?"

When Amane told Itsuki about his shopping trip, his friend looked at him and laughed pretty much the same way the clerk had the day before.

The two of them were eating lunch together in the cafeteria, and when the topic of White Day came up, Amane had spilled the beans.

"Geez, keep it down!" Amane insisted. "Anyway, I was worried that giving her an accessory might weird her out, since we're not dating."

"You're such a coward! A man should have more nerve, more spirit! And anyway, I have a feeling that she'll be happy with anything as long as it comes from you, ya know?"

"...I guess so, but..."

Mahiru was the kind of girl who would graciously accept any gift, but Amane wanted to give her a present that she would genuinely enjoy and want to use, so he had been stressing out trying to choose something good.

"So what did you end up buying?"

"…A rose-gold bracelet with a flower pattern."

He had thought that the soft warmth of the rose gold would suit her better than cool-looking silver or extravagant yellow gold. Of course, he was just in high school, so he couldn't afford real precious metals, so it was only gold-plated, but he had been careful to select a design that seemed to suit Mahiru's style.

"Really? That seems like exactly the kind of thing she'll like, man."

"…She won't be weirded out?"

"No way; you're worrying too much. Why are you always so negative about this stuff…?"

"She's the only girl I've ever seriously thought about giving a present to."

His mother didn't count, and he wasn't thinking of Chitose, either. And anyway, he'd only gotten Chitose a confection that he already knew she liked, so that present felt like it was on a different level.

"You really don't have any confidence with this stuff, huh…?"

"And why should I? I mean…it's Mahiru!"

"She was happy with the teddy bear, right?"

"Well, that's true, but—"

"Amane, it's all about feeling, man, feeling. You've already spent the cash and chosen the gift, so all that's left now is to put some emotion behind it." Itsuki made it sound so simple.

"If it was that easy," Amane grumbled, "I wouldn't have any problem." He pressed a hand to his forehead.

It seemed he would be plagued with doubt over his decision until White Day.

When the fateful day arrived, Amane was waiting for Mahiru in his apartment, wearing an unusually nervous expression. The mood at school had reminded him of Valentine's Day. The boys who had come out on top a month earlier were anxious about giving their return gifts, and the girls were waiting with barely contained anticipation.

Incidentally, Yuuta had faithfully returned each and every gift, repaying each one with an identical box of sweets. Amane's eyes glazed over when he considered that even doing the very minimum must have cost Yuuta tens of thousands of yen.

In any case, there was no way that Amane would have given Mahiru his present at school, so now he waited for her to arrive at his apartment.

He had rushed home from school to compose himself, but try as he might, he was just not used to giving gifts. His nerves were threatening to get the better of him.

Just this once, he wasn't wearing his usual sweatpants and T-shirt, but rather a layered outfit with a gray V-neck sweater over a white shirt, paired with chino pants. He'd tried to look a little less sloppy than usual, but he wasn't entirely sure how his new look would be received.

Amane was still struggling to get ahold of himself when he heard the sound of the front door unlocking. He sat bolt upright, startled.

It was Mahiru, using her duplicate key, as usual. When she came into the living room, she looked at Amane and froze.

"Ah, wh-why is your hair like that?"

"Well, uh, it is White Day, ya know, and I wanted to dress up a little, so I thought I had better try to clean up my act today... If you don't like it, I can go fix it, though."

He'd obviously succeeded in surprising Mahiru, and she didn't seem to be taking it too well—but when he stood up, she waved a hand in front of her face.

"Th-that's not what I meant. I was just surprised, is all."

"I see."

Amane could tell that something was up with Mahiru. He was starting to think he should have stuck to his usual getup.

Mahiru was fidgeting as she took a seat beside him.

"…You still look uncomfortable. Should I go change?"

"N-no, it's fine, it's just… It's a lot."

"What do you mean?"

"W-well, you're always so low-key. I feel like I can relax around you. But…when you're all done up like that, it makes it hard to stay calm."

"In that case, I'll take it off."

Mahiru grasped his sleeve tightly. "…I said it's fine."

When she looked up at him with dewy eyes and flushed cheeks, Amane felt his heart leap in his chest. He knew she wasn't doing it on purpose, but she was really making it hard for him to maintain his composure. It didn't help that she was close enough that he could smell her sweet perfume.

Amane was incredibly aware of the way she was fidgeting restlessly and how tightly she was holding on to him. Now both of them were blushing, and it made the situation even more uncomfortable.

Amane's eyes darted restlessly around the room. "Well, uh, okay," he stammered. Then, in an effort to move past the awkward moment, he gracelessly thrust a paper bag toward Mahiru. "Here. It's your gift. Don't expect too much."

"…Thank you. May I open it?"

"Okay."

It would be embarrassing for her to open it right in front of him, but he wasn't going to say no. Amane had purchased a small box lined with velvet to hold the bracelet, but now he worried that it was too much for the gift he'd chosen.

Mahiru's slender white fingers gently opened the dark-blue box.

Inside was the rose gold bracelet he had purchased the other day, as well as some folded paper he had included as a bonus.

Mahiru didn't seem to be into gaudy accessories, so he had emphasized elegance and simplicity when choosing the flower bracelet.

Here and there it was decorated with sparkling glass crystals that caught the light and glittered. The design was both cute and refined.

Mahiru's caramel-colored eyes gazed for a long time at the brilliance of the rose-gold bracelet in the box.

"You don't like it...?"

"No, I think it's lovely."

"That's a relief. I picked that because I thought it would look good on you."

"...Thank you very much."

Mahiru's eyes were downcast, as though she was embarrassed by what he had said. Watching her, Amane felt his breath catch in his throat.

"...And this is?" Mahiru asked, noticing the paper he had included in the box.

Amane wanted to look away, but he couldn't take his eyes off Mahiru.

"Ah, that?" Amane scratched his cheek in embarrassment. "Well, um, I kinda thought the bracelet wasn't enough somehow, so... You're always taking care of me, and um, I want to be able to grant any requests you might have, so..."

The paper he had put in the box as a bonus gift was a booklet of *I'll do anything you say* tickets, like the kind a small child might make. The bunch of tickets was good for three uses and featured a hand-drawn illustration of a bear. Amane thought it had turned out rather well, given his skills anyway.

Since Mahiru was always looking after him, he wanted to do what he could to help her out whenever she might need it.

That was the idea behind the coupons anyway, but Mahiru seemed more focused on the illustrated bear. Her shoulders trembled with laughter.

"Pfft-ha-ha, did you draw this yourself, Amane?"

"Oh hush," Amane said sullenly. "I'm no artist. So what?"

"No, I think it's great. You chose it for a reason." Mahiru's innocent smile made it obvious that she hadn't really meant to criticize. "...So can I use them right away?"

"On what?"

Amane hadn't expected her to want to exercise her privilege so suddenly, but if Mahiru had a favor that she wanted to ask of him, he intended to grant her request to the very best of his ability.

Mahiru gently turned the box containing the bracelet around to face him. "...Amane, please help me put this on."

"Oh, come on, you don't need a ticket to ask me that," he said with a troubled smile as he listened to her modest request. "Now, if the lady would allow me to assist..."

Mahiru held out the box, and his expression softened when he saw how cute she looked. After he took the box from her, he set it down on his knees and removed the bracelet, noting the smooth sound of the delicate chain sliding across the velvet. Gingerly, he opened the clasp and gently wound the chain around her wrist. Finally, he carefully fastened it back together. The warm rose gold sparkled on Mahiru's delicate wrist.

I was right, this color does suit Mahiru's light skin.

Since hers was a refined sort of beauty, Amane had guessed that something conservative and elegant would suit her better than something flashy, and he felt a surge of pride when he realized that he had made the correct selection.

"Yeah, that looks good."

"...Thank you."

Thinking it wouldn't do to hold on to her for too long, he let go of her hand, and Mahiru brought the arm bearing the bracelet up to her chest, holding it gently, and smiled softly.

That sweet, unabashed smile, the soft shape of Mahiru's lips, the slight flush on her innocent cheeks... It was both childish and womanly, guileless and refined. Amane found he couldn't turn away from her, no matter how hard he tried.

...This is too much...

Knowing that he was the reason for Mahiru's smile was almost more than he could stand. Amane tried to tear his eyes away and bring his soaring heart back down to earth, but in the end, he kept staring at her until she noticed and hid her face in a cushion.

"So how was White Day?"

The following day Itsuki asked him for a report. Amane did his best to give him a humorless scowl.

Itsuki had been considerate enough not to ask while they were in school, but on the way home, they stopped at a fast-food joint, and the moment they sat down, he began digging for details with a grin.

Amane had only come to eat some fries because he was craving something salty.

Now he thought it probably would have been better not to come if he was going to have to put up with this kind of questioning.

"What's there to tell...? I just gave her the bracelet like normal."

"And was she happy to get it?"

"...More or less," Amane answered in the calmest voice he could muster.

True, he hadn't gotten quite the reaction he'd been expecting, but judging by her earnest smile, he was sure she'd been happy with the gift.

Amane felt a little uncomfortable just recalling that sweet,

©Hanekoto

beautiful smile. He tried to suppress the warmth creeping onto his face.

"Sure, sure." Itsuki folded his arms and nodded knowingly. "I can tell from your reaction that it went over really well. She was definitely happy to get the gift, and she smiled at you really cute-like, right?"

"I mean—" Amane bit his lip.

"Look, man. You're building a solid connection, right?"

Rather than teasing him, Itsuki was speaking earnestly and in a serious tone. Itsuki never intruded in certain areas that, as Amane's best friend, he knew better than to touch. But aside from those topics, he had an uncanny knack for pointing out the truth, so much that it was sometimes uncomfortable. Amane had no recourse—Itsuki's relationship was too well established to make good conversation material at this point, so changing the subject was near impossible.

Amane choked on his words, and Itsuki smiled at him calmly. The somewhat warm look in his eyes irritated Amane.

Seeing there was no use fighting back, Amane snatched a french fry and stubbornly looked away.

Itsuki smiled teasingly at his friend. "I'm happy for you, man. Finally, my little Amane is starting the springtime of his youth!"

"That's not what's happening."

"But you don't know for sure how she feels about it, right?"

"...Even so, I'm sure it's not like that."

Certainly, he knew from firsthand experience that Mahiru trusted him deeply. He wanted to be the person she trusted the most, in fact, and out of everyone she knew in school, he believed that she was the most honest with him.

But that didn't mean they were in love or anything.

Sure, sometimes when they touched, it felt a little...intense. But that wasn't uncommon with opposite-sex friendships. And okay,

Mahiru did do a lot for him, but he was sure that didn't mean she had romantic feelings for him.

And yes, recently Amane had been spending a little more effort on his appearance. But he was still the same hopeless loser he'd always been. There was no way that a girl like Mahiru would fall for a guy like him.

"You know, Amane, you can be pretty pathetic sometimes. Seriously, you're the kind of guy who acts like nobody will ever love him."

"You really think that all it takes for a guy like me to get an amazing girlfriend is a little hard work? I'd have better luck waiting on a miracle..."

"If all the beautiful girls were snapped up by only the most handsome, charming young men of the world, the guys who missed out might go down a violent path, you know."

Amane wasn't sure Itsuki had a right to comment, as a member of the former group.

Itsuki continued, "Anyway, if you insist, we'll leave it at that for now... More importantly, it's time for me to make a prediction as your best friend."

"About what?"

"Sooner or later, you're gonna change. I can already see the telltale signs. All that's left is for you to take the first steps toward your new future."

"...Don't talk like some kind of know-it-all guru," Amane said with a scowl.

"Ha-ha-ha! How long have we been friends?"

"It hasn't even been a year," Amane quipped coolly.

"Oh yeah, that's right!" Itsuki roared with laughter.

The two of them had only known each other since the start of high school, but Itsuki understood Amane much better than the guys he'd known in elementary and middle school back home. He was glad that the two of them got along so easily.

"Anyway—," Itsuki continued.

"Hmm?"

"You keep going on and on about how you're not worthy of her, but your attitude and the way you talk about her just proves that you actually do like her."

"I will stick this french fry right up your nose," Amane threatened.

"Sorry," Itsuki instantly apologized.

Amane came very close to actually being impressed by what his friend had to say only for Itsuki to ruin it right at the end with a ridiculous comment.

"You're late today."

When Amane returned home about an hour later than usual, Mahiru came out to greet him in her apron. After his earlier conversation with Itsuki, Amane couldn't help but think that she looked like a newlywed. He told himself that he didn't feel that way about her, so it wasn't fair to indulge in that delusion, and he drove the thought from his mind in a bit of a panic.

"Mm, I had fries with Itsuki."

"…Right before dinner?"

"Don't worry, I'll finish my plate."

He had a second stomach for Mahiru's cooking, and he had been conservative and only had a small order of fries anyway, so he had plenty of room for his meal, even if Mahiru dished up his usual serving size.

"For a second, I worried about you gaining weight…," Mahiru mused. "But you're so slim that you could probably stand to put on a little bit more meat."

"You're one to talk. I'm always worried you might snap in half one day."

"I'm not that fragile, you know."

"Oh really? Look at how thin you are."

Mahiru had a very slender and feminine physique. Of course, she did quite a few sports, so she wasn't just thin, she was also toned and flexible. Still, she had a delicate look to her for some reason, and just as a test, he reached out and grabbed her wrist, easily wrapping his fingers all the way around. He remembered his father warning him to always treat a lady gently and with care.

She seemed so dainty and thin, he thought, as he moved his fingers along hers, feeling the delicate bones beneath her skin.

Mahiru squirmed uncomfortably. He saw she was staring at her hand in his, her cheeks slightly flushed, and realized much too late that he had been touching her without her permission.

In a panic, Amane released Mahiru's hand.

"Sorry. I should've known you wouldn't like that."

"It's... Well... I don't hate it when you touch me."

Amane stared at Mahiru in shock. He could barely believe his own ears. Mahiru also seemed to realize what exactly she had said and looked up suddenly, cheeks redder than he had ever seen them, eyes beginning to fill with tears. Amane felt like he couldn't possibly bear the embarrassment a moment longer.

"Th-that doesn't mean that I'm asking you to touch me or anything, all right?" Mahiru explained. "Just that I hate it when *other* guys touch me. You understand?"

"Y-yeah," Amane said meekly.

However, his heart was still pounding wildly. The very particular phrasing she had used left an awful lot open to interpretation. He felt like he needed to change the subject.

"…Oh, um, I noticed…," he mumbled, "you're not wearing the bracelet I gave you yesterday. I mean, obviously you don't have to wear it if you don't want…"

Mahiru looked down at her wrist and with one finger softly traced the place where Amane had grasped her.

"…If I wear it when I'm doing housework, it gets in the way, and it'll get damaged sooner… I want to keep it nice, so I'll wear it on my days off."

"…I see."

Amane could not imagine a more perfect answer. She had told him both that she was going to treasure the gift and that she was intending to wear it regularly. His legs threatened to give out on the spot, and his chest felt like it might burst with all the feelings bubbling up inside him, and in the heat of the moment, he was sure there wasn't a man alive who would have felt any different.

Somewhere in this dizzy state of mind, Amane realized how loudly his heart was thumping. He took several long, slow breaths to try to calm down.

"…As long as you like it, I'm happy."

"I do, and I'm going to take good care of it. Like I do with all of them—the teddy bear, the key holder, and the bracelet. I'm going to use the hand cream without reservation, though." Mahiru smiled slightly, looking embarrassed.

Amane could not take it a moment longer. He quickly kicked off his shoes and darted down the hallway.

"…I'm going to change clothes."

"O-okay. See you when you get back, Amane."

Even though he had come home to his own single apartment, Amane felt like he was being sent off by his new wife. His heart began to pound violently again, and he rushed into his bedroom and promptly collapsed on the floor.

Chapter 8

The Start of Spring Vacation

This is worse than I expected…

Amane stifled a yawn as he watched the distant figure of the school principal up on the stage, giving a stern address. He didn't really care about closing ceremonies or whatever speech the principal had prepared for the occasion. Frankly, he would have rather been napping.

Most of the students around him seemed to share that sentiment. Very few people were actually paying much attention. Everybody else was obviously zoning out.

Still, it wasn't like the students could flaunt their boredom, so Amane put on a serious expression and silently wished for a speedy end to the proceedings as he let the principal's speech flow in one ear and out the other, the minutes slipping past as he pretended to be a model student.

He might have cared about graduation, but this was just the closing ceremony. It didn't really matter.

"…Ah, I'm so stiff."

"The principal's speeches are always so long."

That was the general sentiment as the students returned to their classrooms. Nevertheless, everyone sounded quite lively, probably because two weeks of freedom awaited them after this final homeroom period.

From his seat, Amane watched his cheerful schoolmates who would soon be liberated from their boring classes, and he let out a quiet sigh.

Spring vacation started tomorrow, but how would he spend it?

He had pretty much just seen his parents, so considering how much it cost to travel, he figured he could take a pass on going home. But that left him with an empty schedule.

Even if he thoroughly prepared for next year's classes, he would have a lot of time on his hands. He had considered getting a short-term job, but he hadn't managed to line up anything, and now there wasn't enough time. The only friends he had to hang out with over the break were Itsuki and Chitose.

"Hey, hey, Amaneee—"

Itsuki appeared just as he crossed Amane's mind.

When he turned around, he saw Itsuki wearing an enthusiastic smile...and was immediately suspicious. Itsuki only smiled like that when he had a favor to ask, or when he was about to suggest something foolish.

"What is it?"

"Are you free starting tomorrow?"

"I guess I am."

"Right, right, I thought so. That's good, veeery good."

Still grinning, Itsuki patted the bag that was hanging from the side of his desk. Even though everyone was supposed to have cleared out their lockers and desks the day before, Itsuki's bag was obviously packed full. They didn't even have any classes that day, so the most he could have possibly needed to bring to school would be a pen and maybe a binder, but Itsuki's bag looked like it was about to burst.

"…What's all that?" Amane asked.

"Change of clothes."

"Why?"

"'Cause I'm staying at your place…"

Itsuki put on his humblest, most flattering voice and gave Amane an imploring look. Amane couldn't help but scowl back at his friend.

"Hang on a sec; haven't you ever heard of giving advance notice?"

"Sure I have. Consider yourself notified that I'm coming over, staying several nights, and bringing the party with me!"

"What, you're gonna keep the whole neighborhood up all night? How well do you think that's gonna go over, idiot?"

"Geez, dude, I was only joking… But I am serious about you letting me stay with you."

Itsuki rarely failed to let Amane know ahead of time when he was coming over. The first thing that came to mind was that it was an emergency. Amane struggled to imagine what it could be about, though.

"I had a fight with my dad this morning."

As if to answer Amane's internal question, Itsuki readily disclosed the reason.

"…About Chitose?"

"Yeah. When my dad gets mad, he won't listen to me unless I leave him alone for a few days. And I've been staying at Chi's house a lot, so I'd rather not go there. No matter how accepting her parents are, it doesn't seem right, ya know?"

"But you're okay staying with me?"

"I thought you might let me."

Itsuki probably assumed it would be no big deal. He'd stayed over at Amane's apartment plenty of times, even before Amane had cleaned up the place.

And it wasn't like Amane didn't want to let his friend stay with him. But there was the issue of Mahiru. Amane was worried that he would be forcing her to stay in her public persona during a time when she wanted to relax, since he didn't think she would feel comfortable acting casually with Itsuki around.

And there was another issue. Recently, he had noticed that Mahiru had been acting strangely affectionate, and he was afraid that if Itsuki saw her treating a guy that way, he would immediately get the wrong idea.

"...Let me ask."

Amane sent Mahiru a text message asking her what she thought. She would probably send him a memo about the shopping before going home, so he expected she would see it when she did that. It only took a moment for him to send the message, but Itsuki let out a long, drawn-out sigh.

"What—are you two living together or something?"

"I'll leave you on the floor with no heater or futon."

"Just when I start to think you're a nice guy for letting me stay over, you go and threaten to stand by and do nothing while I freeze to death?"

"Hey, you got yourself into this."

Amane shot a look at Itsuki that essentially said *What are you even going on about*, and Itsuki could only shrug in response.

I'm the one who should be shrugging. I don't want you to cause Mahiru any trouble with your usual antics.

Itsuki was pretty good at reading the room, so Amane didn't think he would knowingly bother Mahiru or anything, but he wasn't looking forward to all the teasing he would have to endure the moment she wasn't around. Amane let out a sigh as Itsuki grinned at him.

Apparently, Mahiru sometimes checked her phone at school, because Amane had already gotten a response: "*I'll make dinner as usual if you buy enough food for three.*"

"She said it's all right."

"Yay, I get to eat Mahiru's cooking!"

"That wasn't your goal all along, was it?"

"Let's just say I'm not one to waste an opportunity. Besides, you're always raving about her cooking. I want to try it at least once."

"...Don't you dare be a nuisance to her."

"I may be a nuisance to you, but never to her."

"Don't annoy me, either."

Itsuki cackled, and Amane flicked him in the forehead. Though his friend yelped in pain, he still wore a giddy smile, and Amane let out another overdrawn sigh.

"So how long are you planning on staying?"

Amane was looking at Itsuki, who had made himself comfortable the instant they'd gotten the shopping through the door. Itsuki hadn't been coming over much lately because Mahiru was always around, but before that, he'd visited Amane's apartment often, and he obviously still felt right at home.

Itsuki crossed his legs and took a sip from his cup of coffee, staring off in thought. He looked like a model in a photo shoot. "Hmm... Well, for now, why don't we say...three days, give or take. Geez, this is a real pain!"

"Your dad's not a bad person, but he does seem to be pretty stuck in his ways."

"The old geezer's a stubborn ass."

"Come on—"

"I mean, what gives him the right to tell me who I can and can't date?! Whatever; I'm moving out once I'm an adult anyway." Itsuki stuck out his tongue in a show of anger.

Amane knew that Itsuki didn't actually hate his father. His old man was the kind of guy who had to have everything his way, sure, but once somebody won his affection, he always treated them well. Amane thought he was a good person at least.

But Chitose had never obtained his approval. Amane thought that it probably had to do with the fact that Itsuki's family was fairly well-to-do. Itsuki's father probably wanted his son to date someone from the same social class. At the same time, Amane wondered if maybe Itsuki's father just couldn't stand Chitose's unique personality.

Either way, it sounded like he had dismissed Itsuki's relationship without listening to anything Itsuki had to say. So Itsuki had declared that, if that was the case, he was leaving home.

"You've got it good when it comes to parents, Amane. They let you do whatever you want."

"My parents are super close, so I guess they want their son to choose a partner he likes."

"I am seriously jealous of your parents."

Itsuki's upbringing had been really strict, so perhaps it was only natural for him to be going through a rebellious phase. Bleaching his hair and acting like nothing ever bothered him were just other parts of his insurrection. Amane didn't think he was really in a position to criticize.

"You say that, but I'm sure your parents can't be that bad."

"They might be decent people, but they're awful parents. I mean, you can't just try to control your kids all the time, man. You gotta let 'em run free sometimes, 'cause if you always try to keep 'em on a leash, they're gonna bite you one day."

"And you think you'd be okay, running wild all the time?"

"Maybe, if they'd let me do my own thing. But instead they slapped a collar on me and put me in a cage, so all I can do is bare my fangs." Itsuki shrugged. "They've been alive for how long? You'd think they would have learned better by now." He slurped down the rest of his coffee in one go.

"Well, you can relax for a few days. I mean, we're on break, so we've got nothing but time."

"Friends truly are life's greatest treasure…!"

"Don't cling to me like that; it's creepy."

"You wound me! I demand Lady Shiina's cooking as consolation!"

"As if you need an excuse to eat dinner…"

"Tee-hee!"

"Don't act like such a weirdo."

"How cruel, to wound me yet again! Oh, boo-hoo!"

Itsuki pantomimed wiping away tears, but his grin was wider than ever. Amane watched him with exasperation but also a small sense of relief.

Itsuki had frequent battles with his father, but the fight this morning seemed to have gotten to him more than usual. It was obvious that he'd been putting on a brave face at school.

Amane was glad to see that his friend was feeling at least a bit better. Of course, he didn't want to let on to Itsuki that he was worried about him, so he pretended to be sour even as he secretly breathed a sigh of relief.

Mahiru came over to Amane's apartment sometime after sundown.

She arrived empty-handed, presumably because Amane had already acquired all the ingredients she had requested.

Amane had given her advance warning that his friend would be there, so she didn't seem put off by the sight of Itsuki making himself at home. In fact, Itsuki was the one who seemed slightly flustered.

"It's been a while, Akazawa."

"Nice to see you after so long. Sorry to suddenly barge into your love nest… Ow, owww! I get it; it was only a joke! Sorry to suddenly intrude; it must be awkward for you to have some unfamiliar guy hanging around."

Amane had wordlessly stomped on Itsuki's foot, but even as he groaned in pain, he wore an amiable grin.

"No, not at all," Mahiru replied. "It's fun to have such…lively people over."

"Well, don't expect any peace or quiet with this guy around," Amane added.

"You shouldn't say things like that," Mahiru scolded.

Amane held his tongue, but Itsuki was giving him a smug look, so he pinched him on the side where Mahiru couldn't see. Unfortunately, Itsuki was in very good shape, so there weren't many places where he could find purchase with his fingers.

"Well then, I'm going to go make dinner, so please relax."

Mahiru ignored the boys' squabbling, flashed her angelic smile, put on her apron, and departed for the kitchen. She was obviously comfortable leaving their guest in Amane's hands.

Itsuki stared at Mahiru's back as she went, still smiling smugly. "…You're close enough to give her a key to your place, huh?"

"Shut up."

Mahiru had let herself in with her key, rather than buzzing over the intercom. Itsuki had not failed to pick up on this sign of intimacy.

"And she told me 'Please relax' like she runs the place. Honestly, she's acting like she's already your wife!"

"Do you want me to kick you out?"

"Okay, okay, I'm only kidding…is what I'd normally say, but you gotta understand how this looks, my man!"

Amane tried to grab him by the scruff of the neck, but Itsuki twisted away. He scuttled across the carpet and booted up Amane's video game console. Amane slid off the couch and sat down next to him, making sure to give him a gentle knee in the back on the way, and the two of them killed some time playing games.

Before too long, Amane started to hear the sound of Mahiru

taking the dishes out. He wasn't going to make her do everything, so he stood up and headed for the kitchen.

"Let me help. Can I take the dishes that are already plated?"

"Yes, thank you."

Amane took several plates piled with food out to the table. When he set them down, he caught Itsuki staring at him, looking dumbfounded.

"...How should I put this...?"

"What's up?"

"Know what? I'll keep it to myself."

"What the heck...," Amane muttered as Itsuki started packing away the game console.

When it was time for dinner, the three of them sat down, with Mahiru's homemade dishes between them, and Itsuki wore a truly pleased expression.

"So good..."

"Thank you very much."

Mahiru sat up straight and proper as she ate. She wore her calm, angelic smile, but since Itsuki already knew their secret, Amane could tell that she was letting herself relax a little.

Itsuki looked like he was in a trance, bringing bites of food to his mouth.

Amane had warned Mahiru ahead of time that Itsuki would eat more than he would, so she had prepared large portions for him, but even so, he was putting it away pretty quickly.

"Wow, you're a lucky man, Amane, to be able to eat food like this every day..."

"I'm all too aware of that. The food is delicious as always, by the way."

"...Thank you very much."

He gave Mahiru his reaction after sipping his miso soup.

Amane's lips curled into a smile as he savored the taste. He couldn't help but grin at the comforting combination of dashi and miso. It was so good that he never got tired of it, even having it every day. But the person who cooked it didn't seem to realize just how sublime it was, so he always made sure to tell her.

The soup had a gentle flavor that reminded Amane of her personality. It warmed him all the way down into his belly. He didn't find it at all surprising that Itsuki was entranced.

"Ah, it's so good."

Today Mahiru had made Amane's favorite dish, rolled omelets, so he had an even bigger appetite than usual. Of course Mahiru's food was so good that Amane always went back for seconds, but even so, his appetite was an entirely different beast when eggs were on the menu.

As he was smacking his lips at the rich, comforting dishes, Itsuki kept glancing over at Amane and Mahiru. "…What a happy couple," he muttered.

"Did you say something?"

"Nope!" Itsuki shook his head. "Not a thing!" He returned his attention to his plate.

Amane decided not to question him any further. He noticed that Mahiru was staring at him quietly and simply shrugged.

After dinner, Mahiru went home early.

Usually, she would stay at Amane's place until it was time to wind down, typically a bit after nine o'clock, but because Itsuki was staying over, she had decided it was best to leave a little sooner. The two of them had been left alone while Amane had done the washing up, and he wondered if that awkwardness wasn't part of the reason she'd left so soon.

When Amane asked Itsuki what they had talked about, he'd said that they'd just made small talk and chatted about Chitose. Amane hadn't questioned his friend any further, but he had a suspicion that other topics had come up.

"Hey, Amane?"

Just before going to sleep, Itsuki looked up from where he had spread out a futon on the floor of the bedroom.

"What is it?" Amane asked from his bed.

"The way you look at Shiina, with those big soft eyes... You definitely have a thing for her, right?"

"Shut up."

"Anybody can see it, man. You're absolutely lovestruck."

"Don't make me kick you out into the cold."

"Aw, c'mon."

Amane shot his friend a glare that dared him to keep going, but Itsuki did not look the least bit discouraged. On the other hand, he wasn't wearing his usual cheeky grin, either. Itsuki's expression looked genuinely happy—and even a little proud.

"Well, fine, I'm not expecting you to admit it. But I want you to know that I'm happy for you, man. I'm happy that you found somebody who can appreciate you."

"Huh?"

"Geez, you really are dense. Look, most of the folks in our class probably think you're a weird, gloomy loner."

"I'm perfectly aware of that, thank you very much."

Among his classmates, Amane had always been something of a plain, unsociable character, the kind of boy who never really stood out or got noticed, despite his high ranking on almost every exam.

Compared to guys like Itsuki, the sophisticated and cheerful gentleman, or Yuuta, the fresh-faced prince, Amane might as well have been invisible. Not to mention that, whether he knew it or not,

Amane was always doing his hardest to not stand out or make waves. Of course he wasn't popular.

"But they're only going by what they can see," Itsuki continued. "They don't know the real you. And even the people who do get to know you have to look hard to see your good parts."

Itsuki was staring at Amane without a hint of mockery in his eyes. His sudden earnestness made Amane a little uncomfortable.

"It's such a waste that you don't know just what an awesome guy you are. That's why I'm so happy that Shiina sees you for who you really are and gets along with you so well."

"Itsuki…"

"So hurry up and start dating her, and let's go on a double date!"

"Geez, why does it always come back around to that?"

While he obviously couldn't pass up the opportunity to tease his friend, Amane noticed that Itsuki wasn't looking directly at him. He was probably trying to hide his embarrassment after getting all emotional. Amane figured Itsuki could stand to be off-balance for a change.

"Chi would be happy, too, ya know," Itsuki added.

"By all means, you two go have the time of your lives. Just leave us out of it. I mean, if—and this is entirely hypothetical—but if we did develop that sort of relationship, would you really want to be seen with a guy who looks like I do?"

"No, we'd obviously get you to transform into the mystery man. Speaking of which, you still haven't let me see it."

"Nope."

"Is it one of those things you only let Shiina see?"

"Itsuki, you have a choice. Either you can shut up and enjoy my hospitality or freeze to death beneath the cold winter sky."

"Well, excuuuse me!"

Itsuki knelt on top of his futon and bowed in mock apology.

"Good grief," Amane muttered in an exasperated tone.

Itsuki must have still been scheming up ways to get his buddy a girlfriend to spice up his life.

But there's no way I have any chance of dating Mahiru...right?

She already did so much for him. If the two of them really did start dating, he would probably come to rely on her for absolutely everything. Forget how spoiled he was now, dating Mahiru was a sure path to utter dependency.

And anyway, Mahiru didn't seem interested in guys.

She didn't have much of a problem being around Amane or Itsuki or even Amane's father, but when it came to the other boys at school, she kept them all at a comfortable distance, wearing her angel mask like thick armor.

Male classmates were constantly approaching her to confess their love, but he'd never known Mahiru to date anyone, ever. It was like she didn't want anything to do with boys.

And since Amane still wasn't sure exactly how he felt about Mahiru, he was in no hurry to embarrass himself with a halfhearted confession. Plus, he was convinced that Mahiru didn't have those kinds of feelings for him anyway.

Dating Mahiru would remain a distant fantasy.

"...But look, Shiina obviously really likes you. Step back and take a good look at your situation before you dismiss it all as impossible." Itsuki spoke as if he had seen straight through Amane's heart.

Amane just mumbled "...Easy for you to say..." and crawled under his comforter.

"Itsuki is so sneaky! I want to eat Mahirun's cooking, tooooo!"

The following day, Chitose called Amane on the phone at a ridiculously early hour. Evidently, Itsuki had been in touch with her the night before. He had taken photos of their dinner, like he had often seen many girls going, apparently for the purpose of sending it to Chitose.

"Don't tell me. You've gotta ask Shiina."

"Okay, so if I get Mahirun to say it's okay, you'll share with me?"

"Uh, well—"

"Got it!" Chitose answered energetically. "Okay, I'm gonna go ask her!"

Then she hung up.

Amane had been holding the phone away from his ear because Chitose was so loud. Now he made an exasperated face. As usual, he wasn't sure whether he should be impressed or terrified by Chitose's energy.

Itsuki, who'd been watching the whole time, looked awfully pleased.

"Chi sounds pretty excited."

"Can't you do something about your girlfriend?"

"Pretty much impossible, man," Itsuki replied cheerfully. "When she sees something she wants, Chi doesn't hold back. That's why I love her so much."

Amane figured that Itsuki's opinion was a little biased, on account of being in love and all. There was a lot to be said for Chitose's abundant energy and the easy way she made friends with almost everyone, and Amane was ready to admit that he often envied those strengths that he so clearly lacked.

For the time being, he decided to heat up the leftovers from yesterday's dinner and have them for breakfast. Silently, he thanked Mahiru for the food and for her future patience dealing with Chitose's call.

"And so here I am!"

Chitose appeared, along with Mahiru, just before lunch. The two of them were carrying shopping bags overflowing with food. Chitose was also wearing a backpack that looked like it might be an overnight bag, and Mahiru was smiling ruefully. They'd obviously met up earlier and gone shopping together. That explained why they were both carrying bags and how Chitose had reached Amane's apartment.

"You got here pretty quick…," Amane remarked.

"I got all excited about the idea of staying over at Mahirun's place!"

"…Wait, what?"

"We are on spring vacation, so I figured, why not? And Mahirun said I could, so here I am!"

Chitose grinned widely and looked at Mahiru for confirmation, and Mahiru nodded with a smile.

She obviously had no choice.

Chitose must have strong-armed Mahiru into allowing her to stay over. But Mahiru didn't seem particularly upset or anything, only somewhat bewildered by the sudden development.

As Mahiru went to put the groceries away in the refrigerator, she leaned close to Amane. "Don't worry about me. I told her it was okay," she reassured him in a whisper so quiet that only he could hear.

Amane wore a worried smile as he watched Mahiru put the dinner ingredients in the fridge.

"I'm looking forward to Mahirun's cooking!" Chitose beamed as she sat down next to Itsuki and clung tightly to his side. Amane had lost his seat for the moment, so he headed into the kitchen.

"Is there anything I can do to help?"

"…Amane, you know you can't cook."

She kept her voice down so it didn't carry into the living room and called him by his first name. Amane smiled slightly.

"I could cut up vegetables or something? Actually, if you give me instructions, I could do something simple. I showed you that I can actually make some things, didn't I?"

"...All right, I'll take the help. You really don't want to stay in the other room, do you?"

"Very perceptive. They're already flirting."

Amane shrugged and moved to the sink to wash his hands.

He knew he couldn't do much, but it wasn't like he was completely useless. He could at least help Mahiru out with things like measuring and prep work, so he turned his back on the lovebirds and their flirting for a while and became Mahiru's kitchen assistant.

"By the way, what are we having for lunch today?"

"Omelets over rice, with green potage soup and a salad. Chitose said that she wanted to eat the type of omelet that's half cooked inside when you cut it open with a knife."

"Nice."

"You really like egg dishes, don't you?"

"Eggs are great. Plus, yours are the most delicious, so I'm already looking forward to it."

Mahiru's cooking never disappointed, and Amane was even more excited to hear they were having eggs, his favorite. He still thought about the beef stew omelets they had eaten that one time. He would have been happy eating those every day.

Amane silently lauded Chitose for her excellent menu request as he cheerfully measured and washed four portions of rice. Gradually, he noticed that Mahiru was still standing there, next to the refrigerator.

"...What's up?"

"...I appreciate the compliment, but don't catch me off guard like that."

"What do you mean?"

"It's fine if you didn't get it."

Mahiru abruptly turned away and began cutting up the ingredients for the soup, leaving Amane standing there looking bewildered.

"I can't believe they can act like that and still not be dating."

"Seriously."

"Ah, that was sooo goood!"

Chitose finished the last of her lunch and patted her belly in utter satisfaction.

Mahiru smiled, glad that her efforts were so appreciated. Apparently, she rather liked entertaining. The day's sudden appearances had evidently not been too trying.

"Wow, you really can make anything, huh, Shiina?" Itsuki gushed. "You were able to prepare half-cooked omelets that kept their shape while still being so soft in the middle."

"It's all thanks to my cooking teacher," Mahiru replied modestly.

"You studied cooking?" Chitose asked.

"Yes, sort of. Enough to take care of myself and to entertain guests when I need to."

"Whoa!" Chitose marveled. "That must have been one amazing teacher if you learned to cook like this!"

Mahiru must have been talking about the maid she had mentioned to Amane before, the only person in her parents' house who had treated her with any kindness.

"I wonder if I could get this good, if I had a teacher like that."

"Maybe if you were a little less...adventurous in the kitchen, you would have better results," Itsuki suggested.

"Hey—what's the point if you don't experiment a little?!"

"Well, if you tried following a recipe for once, I'm sure you could make just about anything."

It was true; Chitose would have made a really good cook if she ever stopped messing around. But her lack of discipline really undermined her efforts.

Chitose's personality was like a cat's—she did whatever she fancied at the moment and generally pursued things at her own speed. The problem was that she had basically no self-control. She could force herself to focus for a while if she had to, but it was obviously exhausting for her. Chitose just wasn't wired that way.

"And not just in the kitchen, either," Itsuki continued. "You could try bringing a little composure to your everyday life. You've got a great role model right there, see?"

"Oh, I'm sure you'd just love me to become more like Mahirun, but I'm afraid you're out of luck. Besides, it seems...uncomfortable."

"That's awfully rude to Shiina."

"Maybe. But you have to admit, Mahirun always seems so formal. Or maybe, like, stifled?" Sometimes Chitose could be surprisingly perceptive. "The Mahirun we see at school is pretty dull."

"...Is that really how I come off to others?" Mahiru murmured.

"Well...we are in different classes," Chitose answered, "so I'm no authority, but you seem dull or...sort of like you're looking down on everything, from a distance, you know? I mean, you're still nice to everyone, but I can tell you never let your guard down."

Chitose's conjecture was right on target.

Mahiru certainly treated others with kindness and respect, but she also never let anyone except for a very small number of people see behind her mask. By playing the part of the gracious and upstanding young woman, she kept her true identity safe and hidden.

Nobody knew that better than Mahiru, though. Amane watched her expression grow cloudy. But Chitose threw an arm around her and smiled.

"Mahirun makes a super-cute face whenever I bring up this kinda personal stuff, so you can tell that she's being honest, right? I like this version best!"

Chitose giggled and squeezed Mahiru tight. Mahiru looked embarrassed for a moment, but then she hesitantly returned Chitose's embrace.

"You know, Mahirun," Chitose continued, "I think you should open up more. I mean, you could have Amane totally spoil you, you know? And we know you can be super sweet to people you like. So if you'd just use that to your advantage, you'd have them eating out of your palm!"

"I will do no such thing!" Mahiru insisted.

"Ehhh?"

"...I'm not like that at all, Chitose," Mahiru muttered, turning away sharply.

"Oh reaaally?" Chitose replied, staring at Amane.

Of course Amane was not about to get involved in this discussion. Mahiru hadn't asked him for help or anything, and he knew that she could fight her own battles.

That said, if she ever did happen to ask, Amane was ready and willing to do just about anything her heart desired. He would help her shoulder any burden and support her however he could. That would be too embarrassing to admit, though, so he tried to maintain a neutral expression as he watched Chitose and Mahiru's exchange.

"Oh man, it's a feast for the eyes to watch two beautiful girls getting along, huh?"

"Your words, not mine."

Letting Itsuki's somewhat perverted remark pass by without comment, Amane realized that Mahiru had found a friend of the same gender. He was glad she had someone else she could be open with.

Chitose's sleepover naturally took place at Mahiru's place.

Amane had expected her to want to stay with Itsuki, but she had said that since he was always staying over at her place, she was happy being with Mahiru, and the two of them headed back to Mahiru's apartment after dinner.

Amane had already known that Itsuki and Chitose were very close, and that Itsuki often spent the night at Chitose's house. There wasn't anything strange about it, but for some reason, he suddenly felt embarrassed to be confronted with the fact that Itsuki often slept at Chitose's place.

Itsuki whispered, "Whatcha imagining over there, gloomy boy?"

Amane stomped on his friend's foot. He was merciful enough not to stomp on his pinkie toe.

"Listen, man, stomping on my feet isn't gonna hide your shame forever!" Itsuki grumbled.

"It's your fault for being such a jerk," Amane muttered as he turned away.

It's not like he'd been trying to hurt him or anything—Itsuki obviously knew that. Neither of them were actually angry over a little playful roughhousing between friends.

"Actually, I've been staying at her place a ton recently. It's started to become kind of the new normal, you know?"

"Yeah, yeah, I get the picture. You can lay off already."

"I thought that kind of talk was standard between guys."

"It's not, and I can do without it."

Amane had no desire to hear the graphic details of his friend's romance, and he knew that when the story was over, and he glared at Itsuki, Itsuki would cackle with laughter and smile back at him cheerfully.

"You really are a herbivore, eh, Amane? Or is it just a lack of experience that's holding you back?"

"I'll knock you on your ass."

"Well, I guess that's exactly why Shiina opened up to you in the first place, huh? She probably wouldn't have gone anywhere near you if she knew you were on the prowl. Good thing, too, huh?!"

Itsuki gave him a thumbs-up and a big grin. Amane shot him a bitter glare, the sort of face he would never have shown Mahiru.

But it didn't seem to have the slightest effect on Itsuki, who merely laughed it off.

Amane was busy furiously scowling at his friend when his anger was interrupted by a cheerful electronic tone from his smartphone—his text message alert. He stopped glowering long enough to check the screen. The message was from Chitose.

Amane opened the messaging app, thinking that she must be asking about tomorrow's plans, and saw that he had one message, and that it included a photograph.

"Look, look, Mahirun is sooo cute! FYI, I got her permission to send this."

There was just that one sentence and an attached photo.

The picture showed Mahiru sitting on top of a bed, holding the teddy bear that Amane had given her propped up on her knees, with what looked like her bedroom in the background. That was not what made Amane pause.

In the photo, Mahiru was wearing pajamas—specifically, a flowing, long-sleeved, light-pink gown, otherwise known as a negligee. She looked elegant and refined—and hypnotically feminine. She had obviously just stepped out of the bath, and the skin peeking from her sleeves and the open collar of her gown was still faintly flushed.

It was an incredibly suggestive image, even though nothing inappropriate was exposed. She somehow looked modest and seductive at the same time.

And what drew his eyes more than anything else was Mahiru's expression. She wasn't looking at the camera. Rather, her head hung slightly, and she kept her eyes downcast—not enough to hide her face, but enough to give the impression of shyness.

The rosy spots on her cheeks were probably not just from the bath.

Mahiru's expression looked shy, but like she was yearning. It was way more enticing than any expression he had ever seen before. But the teddy bear sitting in her lap also made her look even more adorable than usual. It was just a photograph, but Amane could feel his cheeks burning.

—That jerk!

What was Chitose trying to do, sending him a photo like this? Especially right before bed? There was no way he was going to be able to sleep after seeing something like that.

"Why are you blushing?" Itsuki inquired. "You looking at dirty pictures on your phone or something?"

"Of course not!"

"Okay, then what are you looking at?"

Itsuki quickly peeked over his shoulder, and Amane had no time to hide the image. The picture displayed on the screen was reflected in Itsuki's eyes, and he smiled knowingly.

"I see, I see. You really are one innocent boy, huh?"

"How about you go to sleep—forever?"

"Are you implying that you want me dead?"

"Should I say it directly?"

"That's awfully unkind of you. I mean, what man wouldn't get excited seeing an angel like that? Though, I gotta say, Chi's still the cutest..."

"Stop going on about your girlfriend already, stupid."

Amane sighed in exasperation and brushed his hair back with his hand, and when he did, he heard the clicking sound of a camera shutter.

©Hanekoto

"...Itsuki?"

"Nothing; just got a message from Chi telling me to take a picture of you to commemorate the evening. Just a dumb little memento. Should be no problem, right?"

"I guess. As long as you're not planning to do anything with my photo..."

"Relax, it's not like anyone else will ever see it. And besides, there's a good reason for it, I can assure you."

Amane regarded Itsuki with deep skepticism. He had no idea what that reason could be. But Itsuki just smiled, looking particularly smug, and Amane let out a big sigh, grumbling quietly to himself that there was no point in taking his photo.

Listening to his friend complain, Itsuki muttered in an even quieter voice, "This guy really doesn't get it, does he?"

"...I'm exhausted..."

On the third day, Itsuki and Chitose's stay was finally over. The two of them had gone back to Chitose's place, where Itsuki would spend another day or two. (Apparently Chitose's parents would've been perfectly fine if he stayed forever, but all the same, he didn't want to impose.) They'd eaten Mahiru's homemade lunch and left with big smiles, but not before encouraging Amane and Mahiru to play nice in their absence. Amane had figured that quipping back would have been more trouble than it was worth, so he'd let their teasing slide.

"Aren't you tired, too, Mahiru?"

The two of them were sitting together on Amane's couch.

"...I'm wiped out. That was really hard. But it was also a lot of fun."

"Yeah?"

Mahiru wasn't the type to invite friends over to her apartment, at least for as long as Amane had known her, so he thought it was great that Chitose had given her the excuse to do just that.

It sounded like she sometimes hung out with Chitose when Amane wasn't around, so if she had made a close friend, that couldn't be a bad thing.

"...Well, you know, I was really surprised when that photo was sent..."

"Ah, ah, oh that?"

When Mahiru said the word *photo*, Amane couldn't help but recall her elegant yet risqué getup from the night before. His cheeks were burning.

It wasn't like she had bared a lot of skin, but Amane could still remember the way her nightgown had accentuated her soft curves. If anything, her modesty had only made her more enticing. He'd already filed the image away in his mind for later, though he felt surprisingly guilty about it.

"Y-yesterday," Mahiru explained, "yesterday, Chitose said 'You're so cute!' and took a lot of photos. S-so, I'm not exactly sure which one she sent you. She was really insistent, so I gave her my permission, but...I hope it wasn't anything too embarrassing..."

Apparently, Chitose hadn't shown Mahiru which photo she had sent. Amane figured she'd sent him the best shot, but he wondered whether Mahiru was aware how she'd looked—or even that Chitose had photographed that particular moment at all. He wasn't sure how Mahiru would react if he showed her the picture. The photo wasn't obscene or anything, and Mahiru definitely hadn't looked bad, but still, it could cause a lot of trouble.

"Uh, ummm, well, it was...it was a picture of you with the teddy bear on your knees."

"...Th-the teddy bear...?"

"I guess you're taking good care of it, huh?"

Well, that part was true, at least.

Amane, still feeling guilty, decided the best thing to do was shove the image deep down into the recesses of his memory. If he couldn't forget it, he could at least seal it away.

When Mahiru heard the word *bear*, she seemed to more or less recall the moment the photo had been taken, and she smiled slightly.

"...I told you I was going to cherish it," she said, "because it's a precious gift."

Confronted with her warm gaze and soft, welcoming smile, Amane's breath caught in his throat.

This smile was different from her usual angelic smile—it was honest and affectionate. Amane felt hypnotized by her delicate beauty, like her soft sweetness was beckoning him to wrap his arms around her and pull her close.

"...Uh, y-yeah, I guess you did," Amane stammered. "You must really like it, huh?"

"Of course I do," Mahiru replied. "You picked it out for me, after all." She smiled earnestly. "You don't have to worry; I treat him well. Why, every day I pat him on the head, and I hold him tight when I fall asleep, and—ummm...never mind. Forget I said anything."

Amane could hardly believe he'd heard her right.

A beautiful girl like Mahiru sleeps with a stuffed teddy bear. That's unspeakably cute.

He recalled how angelic Mahiru looked when she was asleep. Just imagining the scene made him blush.

Wearing that angelic sleeping face, she cuddles a stuffed bear while she slumbers. Mahiru, this beautiful girl, goes to bed holding the teddy bear I gave her.

Mahiru had already turned bright red, all the way out to her ears. She grabbed him by the arm. "P-please forget about that last part."

"Th-that's literally impossible."

"Ugh, I'm so embarrassed!"

Mahiru looked at him with tears forming in the corners of her eyes. This expression was even more devastatingly cute than the last, but it was obvious that Mahiru didn't realize it.

"Is it really that big a deal? I don't see what the problem is."

"It makes me seem like a little kid, doesn't it? Sleeping with a stuffed animal, I mean."

"N-no, I think it's really cute."

Mahiru turned away from Amane and buried her face in her favorite cushion. "You're not helping..."

Amane felt awfully guilty for thinking that Mahiru looked cute when she was pouting, but he couldn't help himself—he found it endearing.

What he wanted to do right then was reach out and stroke Mahiru's head, but he knew that was a terrible idea, especially now, so he kept his hands to himself and only looked over at Mahiru.

After a few moments had passed, she peeked out from behind the cushion. Her eyes shimmered, and her face was flushed, but she composed herself enough to give him a reproachful look.

"...Amane, you need to tell me something embarrassing, too. It's not fair if I'm the only one."

"What...?"

Mahiru had done this to herself. Amane felt no responsibility to put himself in a similar position. But he knew better than to say that.

On the other hand, he was having a hard time coming up with anything embarrassing that she didn't already know.

"If you won't tell me something," Mahiru said sternly, "I'll just have to message Akazawa and ask him."

"When did you exchange contact info with Itsuki...?"

"Actually, Chitose gave me his information, and we messaged back and forth...yesterday, I think. But it wasn't about anything in particular...nothing you need to worry about anyway..."

Mahiru trailed off and buried her face in the cushion again.

At this point, Amane really had no idea what was going on.

Chapter 9

An Incident and the Angel's Truth

Spring vacation meant quite a lot of free time for those without any particularly involved hobbies. It wasn't that Amane had no interests, he just preferred activities like reading and taking long walks. On occasion, his classmates made fun of him for being so dull.

But Amane wasn't interested in sports or outdoor games. Unless he had somewhere to be, his trips outside were for running or walking, or to go buy groceries, and that was about it. Itsuki had always wondered why Amane didn't appreciate his youth more, but Amane figured he got enough exercise to stay healthy.

Mahiru also didn't seem to go out much. Of course, he sometimes saw her exercising, and she often ventured outside to buy things she needed, but she didn't really go out specifically to do anything recreational.

"Don't you want to go somewhere for fun?"

When he asked Mahiru about it one day after dinner, she looked troubled for a moment, then smiled and answered, "Go somewhere for fun...? Not right now, no. I'm kind of a homebody."

Amane wasn't one to talk, but he wondered whether it was healthy for a beautiful high school girl to stay in all the time. "Well,

I guess I'm the same way, huh? I don't really feel like going out anywhere, either."

"…What about going back to your parents' house?" Mahiru asked.

"I saw them at New Year's, so I think I can take a pass. Plus, I'm supposed to be going home this summer, too. And it would suck to miss out on your fantastic cooking."

"…I-is that so?"

Amane had definitely grown accustomed to enjoying Mahiru's cooking every day. Spending so much time together seemed normal now. He appreciated Mahiru's kindness and her beauty, and he felt calmer just being around her.

"Not to mention, if I go home, they'll just drag me around all over the place, and that sounds exhausting."

"…Drag you around?"

"To resorts and shopping and stuff. If I don't have anything else to do, they take me wherever they want to go. Once when I was in middle school, we even went to hot spring resorts and stuff."

Amane's mother didn't really care whether they were spending time indoors or outdoors—she could get excited about nearly anything as long as she was spending time with family. Whenever Amane didn't have plans, she often tried to drag him with her somewhere. She was usually kind enough to let him choose where they went, but if he let her get away with it, she wouldn't hesitate to take advantage of him.

Amusement parks and shopping malls were charming enough, but Amane's mother also enjoyed mountaineering and airsoft games, which were more intense. Amane had never understood how she contained so much energy in her petite frame.

Thanks to his mother, Amane had learned how to do all sorts of things, and even stayed in decent shape, but it was obvious that his own preference for quiet hobbies was something of a reaction to his mother's riotous enthusiasm.

"…That sounds fun," Mahiru said.

"When it's every single day, you get tired of it pretty quick. I'd rather not start off a new school year totally ragged after trying to keep up with her."

"Ha-ha, I can imagine."

"You'd understand if you came with me. Then she'd focus all her energy on you instead."

"I s-suppose so…"

Amane was sure that his mother would be delighted to go out somewhere with Mahiru. He didn't think she'd want to do anything too hardcore, but she would definitely take her around shopping and stuff.

He knew that his mother had always wanted a daughter and would probably leap at the chance to spend time with any girl right around this age, much less a girl like Mahiru.

"You'll see, if you come to visit over the summer. She'll probably drag you all over the place and treat you like a dress-up doll again."

"…Summer?"

"I have a feeling she's going to ask me to bring you home with me."

By which I mean she's actually already tried to pressure me into it.

As things stood, Shihoko was probably going to approach Mahiru directly by the time summer vacation rolled around.

"Ah, well, if you hate the idea, feel free to decline."

"N-no, I don't hate it! If anything, I'm happy!"

Mahiru shook her head forcefully, and as her hair cascaded around her face, the scent of her shampoo tickled Amane's nose.

"Mm. All right, I'll go ahead and tell Mom. I know she'll be happy to have you over."

"…Thank you."

"I should be the one thanking you for taking some of the burden."

"Oh, please." She slapped his upper arm gently.

Of course it didn't hurt, but Amane's heart started pounding the moment she touched him.

"…Amane?"

"A-ah, nothing, it's nothing."

"You don't really look like it's nothing, but…"

"Honestly, don't worry about it. Oh, look at that. You got a message or something." Amane was all too happy to change the subject. He pointed to Mahiru's phone. It was vibrating and flashing a notification.

Thankfully, Mahiru shifted her attention to the phone. "What could this be?" she muttered as she picked it up and opened the messaging application.

Of course Amane knew it would be rude to read over her shoulder, and he didn't especially want to make eye contact with Mahiru at that exact moment, so he found somewhere else to look, but… when he heard a soft thump, he looked back over to Mahiru and froze.

Mahiru had dropped her phone onto the cushion on her knees and wore an expression like a lost child, as if she was about to cry.

It wasn't just the tears collecting in her eyes or the odd twist in her mouth… She looked like she might shatter if he so much as touched her.

Where have I seen this expression before?

Oh yeah, it reminds me of the first time we spoke.

"…Mahiru?"

"No, it's nothing. Please don't worry about it." Before Amane could even ask her what was the matter, she answered in a rigid voice.

"Now, if you'll excuse me, I've got to be getting home. I have some business to take care of tomorrow, so it seems I can't stay for dinner. I'm sorry."

Mahiru did not give him the chance to argue. She quickly collected her things and left. Amane moved to stop her, but she either didn't notice or deliberately ignored him. He was left reaching out to empty air.

...Why, so suddenly?

He was certain that it must have had something to do with the message she'd received.

As far as Amane knew, there was only one thing that could make her look that way.

"...Mahiru's...parents."

Mahiru didn't give her contact information to very many people, so only a very limited number of people knew her message app ID. There was Amane and his mother, Chitose and Itsuki, and he had heard that a few of the girls in her class who could keep a secret knew it as well. Aside from those people, he deduced that the only other people who might know it were her parents.

He had to assume that the message had come from them.

And suddenly saying that she had business to take care of tomorrow, when she hadn't mentioned anything the day before, must mean that Mahiru was probably going to meet them. He knew she had a difficult relationship with her parents, which explained the gloomy expression he saw just moments ago.

Well, he might have determined the source of Mahiru's consternation, but there wasn't much he could do with that information.

"...Mahiru."

He had caught a glimpse of her face, crumpled and twisted, as she left. He hadn't said anything. Feeling helpless, he quietly muttered her name, letting his fist fall to the cushion that, until just a moment ago, she'd been holding.

The weather was bad that day.

Dark, heavy clouds blanketed the sky, and when Amane looked out the window, he couldn't see a single ray of sunlight. If anything was going to come down from that sky, it would be raindrops.

Perhaps that was the reason it was so chilly, despite the end of March quickly coming up.

Amane turned on the heater and had a seat on the couch, but somehow he couldn't compose himself. Without meaning to, his gaze kept drifting in the direction of Mahiru's apartment.

Today must be the day that she's going to see her parents, huh?

She had already informed him that she wasn't going to make dinner tonight, probably because she didn't want anyone to see her so emotional.

Just remembering what Mahiru looked like wearing such a hurt expression placed a somber, disagreeable feeling in Amane's chest, like the dregs of something dark had collected there.

He was so worried that he nearly sent her a text asking if she needed anything before deciding against it. He was incredibly agitated, but looking around his room, he realized there was nothing he could do, so for the moment, he decided to head to the supermarket to secure dinner.

Even when he was out shopping, no matter what he did, Amane couldn't get the image of Mahiru's sad expression out of his mind. He imagined how painful it must be for her to have to meet her parents, if that was the kind of face she made.

She had looked like she was afraid, he thought, pressing his lips together. Amane tried not to scowl, so that he wouldn't look like some crazy guy, but no matter what he tried, he just couldn't cheer himself up.

Then he dropped a premade entrée into his shopping basket a little too roughly, making it all slosh around, and felt even worse.

Sighing deeply the whole while, Amane paid for his things and slowly walked home under the cloudy sky—and then, when he took the elevator to his floor, he got a strange feeling. Just as he was about to step out into the hallway, Amane paused, lingering in the shadows of the elevator.

There were two people standing in front of the door to Mahiru's apartment.

One of them was a girl with familiar flaxen hair—it was Mahiru.

And the other was a woman he had never seen before.

Even at that distance, he could tell that she was quite beautiful. And she was tall as well, especially compared to the petite Mahiru—by Amane's estimate, she seemed taller than the average man. But her body was undeniably feminine. He could see her ample curves even under her fitted pantsuit and noted that she had an almost perfect figure.

Her medium-length light-brown hair hung loosely down to her shoulders, and she carried herself with unmistakable poise. Her eyes were framed precisely with eyeliner, but Amane didn't think she needed any makeup to look bold and assertive. Even standing facing Mahiru, her stern gaze showed no sign of softening.

She was quite a beauty, but her entire persona was incredibly intimidating. She looked like an extremely capable woman who was impossible to approach under normal circumstances.

Comparing her to the neat and tidy lily that was Mahiru, this woman was like a striking rose. That's how different the two of them were in appearance and temperament.

"Really, you're such a wretched little girl! And you look just like him. There's nothing I hate more."

Amane stared in disbelief as vicious words slithered past the woman's crimson-painted lips. He was sure that this person was Mahiru's mother, but when she spoke to Mahiru, it was with a voice full of scorn. He could hardly believe that Mahiru endured such cruelty at the hands of her own parent.

"At least if you resembled me more it would be a little better... but you had to look like him. Well, it is what it is. Once you graduate, I won't have to deal with you anymore, so there's no point worrying about it now. We can send the necessary paperwork through the mail like always."

"...Yes," Mahiru replied feebly.

The woman snorted and turned on her heel. "This is good-bye, then. And don't bother me with pointless nonsense anymore."

She was heading for the elevator, so Amane didn't have much choice but to step out into the hall. The woman glanced at him briefly as they passed each other but left without saying another word.

Mahiru was still standing there, and when she recognized Amane, her face distorted into a grimace.

"...Did you overhear?"

"Sorry."

He didn't lie. He apologized frankly.

Though he hadn't intended to eavesdrop, he hadn't dared come out of hiding while they were talking. Plus, he hadn't wanted to abandon Mahiru in her current state.

"So that woman was—"

"...Sayo Shiina. My birth mother."

Recently, Mahiru had been acting a lot more affectionate, but right now she was far stiffer than when they had first met, and when she spoke, her voice was stilted and ragged.

"I'll just go ahead and say this," Mahiru continued before Amane could ask. "She's always been like that, so I'm used to it." Her voice was distant and monotonous. "My mother has hated me for as long as I can remember, and it's too late for that to change, so please don't worry about it."

Stress, pain, heartbreak—Mahiru could not hide what she was feeling. Even Amane could see through her brave facade. He didn't stop to think about it—quietly, he took Mahiru's hand as she turned toward her apartment.

He fully believed that his instincts were right this time.

Because if he left her alone like this, it seemed likely that Mahiru's thoughts would head in a bad direction.

She looked at him blankly, then gave him a feeble smile and tried to shake off his hand. But Amane gripped more tightly, determined not to let go. He didn't squeeze too hard but held her slender wrist firmly.

"We're sticking together," Amane declared in the kind of authoritative tone he would normally never direct at Mahiru.

Her face twisted into an awkward smile.

"...Really, it's fine. You don't need to worry."

"Well, I want to be with you."

He knew he was being awfully presumptuous, but he didn't intend to back down now.

He stared at Mahiru, and eventually she flashed him an exhausted smile and stopped trying to pull away.

That was good enough for Amane. He led Mahiru into his apartment and sat her down on the sofa.

Smiling weakly, Mahiru looked like she would blow apart after one stiff breeze. Still gripping her hand, Amane took a seat next to her, then let go of her wrist and placed her palms in his.

Slowly, Mahiru seemed to relax a bit.

"...It's not the best story, but here goes."

After almost ten minutes had passed, Mahiru finally broke the silence.

"My parents didn't marry for love," she said quietly. "They keep the exact circumstances a secret, but they only got married as part of a deal between the two families."

That kind of marriage, based on family interests rather than love and trust, was rarely seen in modern Japan. It wasn't unheard of, but to Amane, it sounded like something out of an old storybook. He knew that Mahiru came from an upper-class family, but...even so, he almost found it difficult to believe.

"And so...the truth is, they never really wanted a child. I was simply the result of one night's indiscretion. Unfortunately, after I was born, they had no choice but to support me financially...but that's all. I don't think they ever had any intention of raising me."

"What do you mean by that?"

"...They rarely ever came home. Even when they did, they just used the house as a place to stay briefly. When I was younger, I hardly ever saw their faces."

Mahiru's voice was quiet and taut. She looked utterly exhausted.

"I can't remember them ever doing anything parental. I was actually raised by our housekeeper. Mother had many affairs and usually stayed with her lovers, and Father was too devoted to his work to have any time for me. He probably had his own affairs as well... Anyway, they gave me plenty of money and left me alone. They said they didn't need a child in their lives. No matter how hard I tried, no matter what I did, they never once looked my way."

Amane finally understood why Mahiru acted like an angel.

She had spent her entire life trying to convince her parents she was worthy of their attention, even if only for a moment, by performing the role of the perfect child, and now she didn't know how to stop being perfect. That or she felt like she had no choice but to hide her feelings behind her angelic mask. Either way, Amane realized that the angel persona had never been something Mahiru took up by choice.

"Ultimately, they never cared. Even though I grew up pretty, even though I got good grades, even though I was good at sports, even though I could do housework…those people never once looked my way. What a fool I was, trying so hard with nothing to show for it."

Amane felt his chest tighten as he listened to her despair.

"And because of my inconvenient existence, they can't even get a divorce. Neither one of them wants to be the one to leave. It would cause trouble both in their family life and at work. They wouldn't be able to expect any support from my grandparents. So they're waiting until I finish university. Once I'm independent, we won't see one another anymore."

"That's…"

"When my mother told me to my face that she didn't want me… it was a shock. I felt so lost. I sat out in the rain in a daze."

That was why Mahiru had been in the park all those months ago, Amane realized. She had been wandering around in pain because of her mother's cruelty. She must have felt like she didn't belong anywhere—that was why she had looked so anxious and hopeless, like a lost child with no one to turn to for help. Not knowing what to do, she had lingered there in the park, alone with her mother's hateful words.

As Amane imagined the scene, he felt the slight taste of iron spread through his mouth. It occurred to him that he had been biting his lip when he recognized the taste of blood. He was having trouble containing his outrage at this tragedy.

"…If I was going to be that much trouble, she could have just not had me."

Her tiny whisper struck him like a stake driven through his chest, pinning him in place. He was so angry at her parents that he could hardly think. Because of their neglect, Mahiru had grown up hiding her feelings, acting like she was strong while she silently agonized behind her mask of angelic perfection. Amane wanted to shout at them, to demand to know how they could treat her this way. But the people who had abandoned Mahiru were not around.

And besides, Amane wasn't sure what he should actually do in this situation.

He was certainly furious at her awful parents, but he was also an outsider, and he didn't think Mahiru would appreciate him poking his nose into her family business. He might just end up making everything worse. When he considered that he might only hurt Mahiru with his reckless words, he decided to hold his tongue.

But it seemed like Mahiru would dissolve into thin air if he left her like this—so Amane took the blanket that was on the couch next to him and wrapped it around Mahiru's shoulders. She looked surprised, but he pulled the blanket over her head and folded her into his arms.

This was the first time the two of them had really embraced, and her body felt tentative and fragile. He was almost afraid that she'd shatter if he squeezed just a little too hard. But it occurred to Amane that the person in his arms had learned that she was supposed to live without relying on anyone.

"Wha—? A-Amane…?"

"…I finally feel like I understand why you are the way you are."

"You mean why I'm so pathetic?"

"No…I mean how you'll try to endure any hardship—and why you never let your guard down."

Mahiru had never been able to rely on anyone, but she had refused to let that break her. The maid had provided what help she could, but she was only an employee, not family. Mahiru had learned to persevere in life on her own, and she had obviously gotten quite good at it.

"Look…I'm not going to interfere with your family situation," Amane said. "I know better than to stick my nose into other people's business."

Amane was an outsider. There knew it was best to respect the depths when it came to complicated family relationships. However, that was not the same as saying that he wasn't going to support Mahiru.

"…But if you need to cry or anything, go right ahead. I'll even pretend like I can't see you. It must be suffocating to have to suffer through such awful stuff."

He didn't actually want to make her cry, but if she kept bottling it up like this, at some point, she would crack.

So he wanted her to let out all her frustrations, everything she was holding back, and cry if she needed. And he would be there by her side if she needed him, too.

He couldn't do much other than support her.

Amane wondered if he wasn't being too presumptuous, but as Mahiru wriggled in his arms and buried her face in Amane's chest, all that apprehension disappeared.

"…Will you keep it a secret?" she asked in a small voice.

"I can't see you, so I know nothing."

"…All right then, just for a little bit…let me lean on you," she mumbled. It was the first time she had ever asked him for support.

Amane didn't respond—he felt like he might be the one to cry if he tried. Instead, he just pulled the blanket farther up over Mahiru's shoulders and held her tight.

"…Promise you didn't look?"

Mahiru hadn't cried for long, maybe ten minutes, tops.

It would have been great if she could have cried enough to get

©Hanekoto

out sixteen years' worth of anguish, but that seemed like more than her body could handle right now. If she added physical fatigue to her mental stress, her brain would probably just shut down.

Mahiru's cheeks were wet when she lifted her face, but she seemed to have recovered a little of her spirit, because when her eyes met Amane's, her gaze did not waver.

"Well, you were leaning up against me, so I couldn't really see much. I definitely didn't see you crying or anything."

Mahiru had slipped off the blanket and smiled gently.

"...Amane?"

"What is it?"

"...Thank you."

"I don't know what you're talking about," Amane replied, looking in the other direction. He didn't feel like he'd done anything worth thanking him for.

Mahiru buried her face in his chest again.

"Let me stay here a little bit longer, please."

"...Sure."

It wasn't like he could push Mahiru aside when she was in this state even if he wanted to. Besides, he wanted to support her however he could. Calmly, he put his arm around her again and gently stroked her hair.

If nobody else will tell her how wonderful she is, I'll do it myself, Amane thought. He wanted her to feel like she didn't have to try so hard anymore. Like she could relax, now that she was with him.

Mahiru must have calmed down somewhat. When she looked up at Amane, she didn't seem so upset. But she didn't look especially cheerful, either. She probably still had a lot on her mind.

"...I wonder what I should do now," Mahiru mumbled quietly. She gave a troubled smile as she looked into Amane's eyes.

"I can try my hardest all I want, but my parents won't even look at me. Even if other people heap on the praise, call me an angel and whatever else, that doesn't mean a thing. Sure, the Mahiru Shiina that they all know, the angel, is idolized and popular, but...nobody cares about the real me. And the worst part is that it's all my fault. I set myself up this way." She smiled bitterly and grasped the fabric of Amane's shirt tightly. "The real me is cowardly and selfish and dull, and...there's just nothing there to like."

"I like you a fair bit," Amane answered without thinking. Mahiru looked surprised as he continued, "I mean, sure, you're not a hundred percent perfect all the time, but I really do think you're charming, and I always admire your honesty. You're being too hard on yourself." He reached out and tapped her lightly on the forehead. "Besides, if you were as selfish as you said, you wouldn't care about what other people think."

Mahiru looked stunned. But the sorrow had faded from her expression.

Amane just couldn't understand why Mahiru was always putting herself down. Surely anyone could see for themselves that she was a hardworking person and a tenderhearted girl. She was honest but considerate, and though she had called herself cowardly, Amane knew that Mahiru had been hurt so much before that it made sense for her to assume a defensive posture by default.

And besides, if she really was so dull, why was Amane always agonizing over her?

He only wished she knew how much more charming she was when she was her honest self with him.

"Don't put yourself down like that," Amane said, gazing into Mahiru's caramel-colored eyes. "After all, there's someone right here who has seen the real you and adores you."

Mahiru was convinced that nobody loved her. That must have been why she had no confidence. But Amane wasn't the only person who liked her—even Chitose had grown really attached to her. Mahiru was obviously wrong about herself.

She looked away from Amane, and her cheeks started to turn red as she pulled herself into a ball. Amane realized what he had said and began to blush as well.

"I—I mean, Chitose and everybody thinks so, too! So don't get the wrong idea," Amane explained frantically. "But anyway, it's not just me. My parents, and Chitose and Itsuki, too—they all saw the parts of you that aren't the angel you always pretend to be, and they all still like being around you! Honestly, you're much more...well, I think your personality is much more likable than you think."

Amane obviously hadn't done a good job explaining himself. Mahiru's face was still bright red. Amane had become pretty embarrassed himself—after all, he was the one saying all that stuff.

"So look, if you want to stop trying so hard because your parents are going hate you no matter what, then you're welcome to escape to my house whenever you feel like it. If my folks know the situation, they'll gladly take you in. You can think of it like time to recuperate."

"...Mm."

"My mom and dad have really taken a liking to you, so I think they would probably let you stay for a long time... Actually, they might not leave you alone until you cheer up. None of us can decide for you what you should do about your parents, but we can take care of you until you reach a decision and keep supporting you after."

"Mm..."

Amane was trying his best not to come across the wrong way, but Mahiru started crying again.

"Wh-why are you crying?"

"I just...feel so lucky."

"I dunno; you seem pretty much the opposite to me..."

Maybe Mahiru was blessed when it came to money, but aside

from that, nobody gave her anything. She hadn't received one bit of the love she deserved. Honestly, it was a wonder she had grown up without becoming twisted and bitter.

Someone should take care of this Mahiru. And Mahiru should take care of herself, too. She should take back a little of what no one offered her, he thought.

"...In that case, can I make some requests?"

"What will it be? I'll do whatever I can."

Mahiru smiled a little. "They're things only you can do, Amane," she murmured. "Like, look at me more."

"I already can't take my eyes off you," he replied. "I'm in awe of everything you do."

"Also, hold me more."

He peered down at Mahiru, wondering if that was all.

"I'm already holding your hand."

Mahiru stared at Amane for a moment, then looked bashful.

"For today, hold me with your whole body."

As soon as she finished her sentence, she wrapped her arms around Amane's neck and buried her face in his chest again. Amane was startled for a moment but knew that he mustn't get any rude ideas. He swallowed deeply and once again embraced her delicate body.

Chapter 10

The Angel's Metamorphosis

Mahiru was acting strange the following day as well.

To be more precise, she didn't appear as dejected as she had the day before, nor did she look especially sad. But she was very stiff and seemed wary in a way that was difficult to describe.

Even though he was just sitting beside Mahiru on the living room sofa, Amane felt like she was surrounded by an air of crackling tension. When he tried to so much as glance at her, she practically jumped, squeezing her favorite cushion tight. However, Amane could also tell by looking at the reflection in his smartphone screen that whenever he looked away from her, she stared directly at him.

He wondered why she was acting this way—and soon came to the conclusion that it must be because of what had happened the day before.

...She must still feel pretty awkward.

Yesterday, the two of them had embraced—and even though he had been doing it to console her, he was worried that it was going to cause problems for their relationship. Clinging to him may have been a momentary impulse, and there was a chance she regretted it now that she had come back to her senses.

Recently, they'd had a lot of close, physical contact, but this was the first time she had pressed herself against him so boldly. It was inevitable that she would feel a little rattled afterward.

Though it doesn't seem like she hates me for it or anything.

If she did, he reasoned, she wouldn't be here, in his apartment, sitting next to him.

But whenever he reached out toward her, she pulled away from him.

"...Should I just give you some space?"

"N-no, that's not it."

He had figured it would be best to keep his distance for a while until she had calmed down, and had suggested as much, but Mahiru hurriedly shook her head.

"Th-this is, well… I'm just ashamed because you saw me in such a pathetic state. I cried so hard…"

"Ah… I see…"

Apparently, she was embarrassed by all the tears. He recalled that after her sobs had subsided the other night, she'd chilled the area around her eyes with ice, so it wouldn't swell up. But nothing she did could change the fact that Amane had seen her in that vulnerable state, which seemed to really upset her.

"Well, it didn't really bother me, so—"

"But it bothers *me*. It was the biggest mistake of my life to let you see me like that."

"That's going a little far… Look, if you bottle all those things up, it's obvious that eventually you're going to explode, dummy."

It seemed like Mahiru was about to put on one of her characteristic shows of courage, so Amane sighed, and before she could stop him, he reached out and pinched her cheek. Her skin was soft and supple between his fingers.

Mahiru looked confused and nervous. She stared hard at Amane. "Hey, what are you doing?"

"If you don't let your feelings out, you're going to crack at some point. It's okay to let other people support you, really. If I'm acceptable, then you can depend on me. If you want to cry, I'll cover you up anytime and pretend I can't see you. You need to learn to let other people take care of you a little."

Yesterday, she had let some of what she had pent up come bursting out, but it seemed like there was a lot more where that came from. Criticizing Mahiru for her reluctance, he pinched her cheek hard as admonishment.

If she was to say that Amane was unreliable and that she couldn't depend on him, he would resign himself to that assessment and accept his dismissal. But as long as that wasn't the case, he wanted her to rely on him more and give him a chance to take care of her sometimes. He wanted to be there for her, especially when she had nobody else.

"Yesterday, you nodded like you understood, so why are you backtracking on that now? You can depend on me. You are not alone."

"...Not alone..." Mahiru nodded as she considered his words. She looked positively dumbfounded by the notion that she did not have to endure everything by herself.

Amane ruffled her hair. "I'm always in your corner. If you call them, Chitose and Itsuki will show up, too, as will my parents. That's how many people care about you—about the real Mahiru."

Mahiru had lamented the fact that no one wanted her. But that was in the past. Things were different now. There were so many people who cherished Mahiru and wanted to help her. She had to know how much she meant to everyone.

Mahiru was silent for a little while as she considered what Amane had said. Then, timidly, she looked up at him, with eyes that were searching for reassurance.

"...And you?"

"Hmm?"

"Do you also care about me...?"

Amane's breath caught in his throat for a moment, then he scratched his cheek. "I mean...if we're sitting here together like this, that must mean I care about you quite a lot."

Amane knew he could be pretty aloof. He just wasn't interested in spending a lot of energy on a relationship with somebody unless they were really important to him. But when he did care about someone, he was always willing to go to whatever lengths were necessary to help them.

And he had cared about Mahiru for a long time now.

He wanted to take some of the painful burden off of her delicate shoulders. He wanted her to smile peacefully. He wanted her to be happy—he wanted to *make* her happy.

"...Really...?"

Mahiru mumbled, burying her face in the cushion. Amane figured it must be pretty embarrassing to hear all that out loud. On the other hand, he was the one who'd had to say all that out loud, so if anyone was going to be embarrassed, it was him.

...Though I'm sure that Mahiru won't take it the wrong way.

He was really worried she might think he was trying to take advantage of her vulnerability. Obviously, if that's what she thought, their time together would quickly end.

Fortunately, Mahiru didn't seem to have noticed Amane's anxiety. She slowly lifted her face out of the cushion and glanced up at him.

"...Amane?"

"What's up?"

"W-would you, um, turn and face the other way?"

"Huh? Why?"

"D-don't worry about why…"

He was confused as to why she was suddenly asking him to turn around, but he obediently turned his back to Mahiru.

He was waiting anxiously, sitting cross-legged on the sofa, when he felt something soft and warm press against his back. That was enough of a surprise to make Amane go completely stiff, and when her slender arms wrapped around his chest, he was practically petrified.

Mahiru was obviously hugging him from behind. At the moment, Amane was grateful that she wasn't doing it from the front.

"…Uh, Ma-Mahiru…?" Amane stammered, feeling his heart pounding in his chest.

She stirred slightly, still clinging to his back. "…So about yesterday…thank you very much. I wanted to tell you again how grateful I am."

Maybe that was why she was holding on to him this way. It was easier for her to thank him if he wasn't looking right at her.

"O-okay…"

"…You've given me so, so much, Amane."

"B-but I really didn't do anything special…"

"You may think it's not important, but it's a big deal to me. So again, thank you."

"…Sure."

"I'm so glad to have you by my side. I'm not sure how well I could deal with everything if I had to face it alone."

"…Oh?"

This was probably Mahiru's way of showing him that she cared.

Amane was happy that Mahiru felt like she could lean on him. He put his hands over hers, wanting to let her know that he had no intention of leaving her alone. When he did, her whole body suddenly shuddered.

Realizing that he had probably gotten too carried away again, Amane pulled his hand away in a panic, but Mahiru explained in a voice that was muffled because her face was slightly buried in his back. "I-it's okay; I was just surprised..." One of her hands roamed around, trying to find Amane's again.

Feeling relieved, Amane grasped Mahiru's hand, and this time she squeezed him back. Amane shivered in surprise, and when he did, he felt Mahiru's head press against his back.

"...Weren't you going to be the one holding me?"

"I-if you're okay with that..."

"You're the only person I would ever do something like this with, Amane," she said sweetly. "The only one."

Amane stiffened again. He felt Mahiru trying to bury her face in his back. She must have been pretty embarrassed after her sudden confession. Even so, Mahiru didn't let him go, and he felt like she must trust him a great deal, and that made him so self-conscious he wanted to tear his own heart out. In fact, Amane was sure he was even more embarrassed than Mahiru was.

Eventually, Mahiru seemed to calm down, and once again she squeezed Amane's hand tightly.

"...A-anyway, like you promised...please see me for who I really am. Never take your eyes off me."

"S-sure. But I...uh...can't really see you right now..."

"Well, if you looked at me now, I'd get mad."

"O-oh, of course... Well, I definitely cannot see you when we sit like this, so...I guess you can relax."

He knew she was probably trying to hide her embarrassment, so he obediently followed her instructions. More importantly, trying to take a peek would just upset her.

Besides, Amane thought, covering his face with his free hand, *it's better if she doesn't see me right now, either.* He let out a quiet sigh. *...At this point, it would be weirder if I* didn't *fall for her.*

"The new semester is starting soon, huh?"

It was several days after Mahiru's tearful revelation. She seemed totally back to normal—she wasn't acting tense or stealing awkward glances at him or anything. And when she looked up from the textbook she was reading and muttered to Amane, it was like she had just remembered what day it was.

Since their talk, the two of them had gotten even closer. Maybe it was because they were reading from the same book, but there were probably currently only two or three hands' worth of open space between them. They were close enough that Amane could feel Mahiru's warmth and smell the sweet scent coming off her. From time to time, something soft would bump into him.

Amane was only just barely holding it together.

"G-guess it does, y-yeah. Once this weekend is over, it'll be a whole new semester. Kind of depressing that there'll be a class change."

"In what way...?"

"I'm not good at making friends, so once Itsuki's gone, I won't have anyone to hang out with."

Mahiru looked surprised. "How can you be so sure of that...?"

"Don't get me wrong, I can carry on a normal conversation as good as the next guy. But I never get past being acquaintances, that's all."

Amane sort of knew how to talk to people all right, but that wasn't the same as making friends. He just felt like his personality didn't have much to offer, and he certainly wasn't particularly charming, so he'd usually had trouble making friends. He had always been more of a background character anyway.

But he was the type of person who was just fine on his own, and if he was separated from Itsuki, that was just the way things went and couldn't be helped. He would simply spend the year on his own.

"...You don't ever take the first step forward, do you, Amane?"

"Uh—"

"You're a good person. I think it's a shame that you don't know anyone outside of Itsuki and Chitose. People would like you if they just got to know you a little, so you should really dial back the whole aloof and indifferent act. There's no reason to keep everyone at arm's length all the time. It's a waste of potential." She reached over and brushed his bangs out of his eyes.

Amane felt intensely embarrassed and tried to looked anywhere else instead of at Mahiru.

"...I don't really want to get to know a lot of people, is the thing. I think I'm good with being close to a very limited number of people."

"Why do you feel that way?"

"Why...?"

That seemed obvious to him.

—I'm afraid of being betrayed. Like I was in the past.

Amane thought it was best to only get close to people he was absolutely sure he could trust. That was how he had come to his current social standing.

"...Well, I don't really need anyone else. As long as I've got you, I'm good."

"...Huh?"

"W-wait, that's not what I meant! I was thinking more like, I'm happy as long as I've got my close friends, including Itsuki and Chitose, too. I don't want a lot of excitement in my life," Amane explained at light speed. He didn't want her to get the wrong impression...even if that impression would have been more accurate than he wanted to admit.

Mahiru was looking at him with an expression of mixed relief and absolute bewilderment. Her cheeks were turning red. Apparently, she had gotten the wrong impression after all.

"...So you also depend on me, Amane?"

"You're, like, the only thing holding me up, in more ways than one."

"When you say it that way, it sounds like I'm quite important in your life, you know."

She said it like she was criticizing him, but her tone of voice was gentle. She looked at him with a gaze that said *What a hopeless guy.*

Amane was grappling with some very complicated feelings, so he scratched his cheek and tried to change the subject. "Well anyway, how are you feeling about the new classes? Are you looking forward to the change?"

Mahiru blinked several times, then relaxed into a smile. "I am looking forward to the class changes."

"Well, I guess you'll survive no matter which class you end up in, huh?"

"That's true, but I'd rather do more than survive. Wouldn't you?"

"I guess you're right."

Getting along with people on a superficial level didn't mean that Mahiru would actually be happy. But she was the kind of person who had to maintain a perfect facade no matter how exhausting that could be.

On the other hand, there was a chance that Mahiru and Chitose would be in the same class. That would give Mahiru the chance to spend more time with a friend who had seen her true nature. It seemed like the best outcome.

"Amane, do you know why I'm looking forward to the class changes?"

Amane was startled to see Mahiru wearing a slightly impish smile, and he put a hand to his mouth as he pondered the question.

"...Because there's a chance you'll be in the same class with Chitose?"

"Okay, well there's that, too...but it's not the right answer, you dummy," she teased.

Amane knew she wasn't trying to insult him, but he could hear a slightly peevish tone in her words, so he decided he'd better humor her for the time being. He stroked her hair, careful not to mess it up. "That's me, a big dummy," he said ruefully.

"...You're awfully sly, Amane."

"Wh-what do you mean?"

"It's okay; you don't have to understand. Just...please don't forget about me once the new semester starts, all right?"

Suddenly, Mahiru shifted, leaning against him with all her weight. He struggled to keep his heart from leaping out of his chest at her.

...What are you trying to do, Mahiru?

It sounded almost like Mahiru was planning something. Amane suddenly had a bad feeling about the next week's opening ceremony. He'd been hoping that the coming semester would be a peaceful one.

You Are Not Alone

The day before the start of the new semester, Amane was slovenly sprawled out on his sofa, lazily watching the news on television.

He was feeling carefree despite the upcoming school year, both because the weather had settled down into the perfect climate for napping, and because no matter what class he was assigned, he knew his social standing wouldn't change.

Through eyes blurry from yawning, he stared at the TV, where a serious-looking announcer was reporting on the best times to see the cherry blossoms. The broadcast covered where the viewing was currently best, how many people were expected to go out to see the trees, and which regions were in full bloom. It all sounded very lively.

Apparently, the region he was living in was close to full bloom, too. According to the news report, the flowers had blossomed quite early this year. It was a surprise to see them out before the start of the new semester. It reminded Amane of his hometown, actually, where they usually bloomed this time of year.

Cherry blossoms, huh…?

Amane had never really cared about the changing of the seasons all that much, but he could understand why some people found it charming. He did have some fondness for the cherry blossoms and liked to see the pale petals.

Come to think of it, there was a row of cherry trees not that far from here, near the river...

Amane slowly sat up.

I really loafed around over spring break, huh? I guess I shouldn't be surprised...

Aside from a moderate amount of weight training and some light jogging, he hadn't gone anywhere or done anything.

Amane had always preferred the indoors, but he'd basically spent the entire holiday sitting in his apartment with Mahiru, so he figured it would probably do him some good to go outside for a change.

He was annoyed that it had taken a news report to get him moving, but today was the last day of spring break, so if he didn't seize this opportunity, he would have to wait a whole week. Really, he had no choice but to just go for it—no time like the present, after all.

Amane rolled off the sofa and changed into appropriate street clothes. He was going alone, so he didn't bother getting into mystery man mode.

Since he was just one lone guy, getting ready was simple. After he changed, he grabbed his bag, stuck his phone and wallet inside, then prepared to leave.

Just as Amane opened the door, a ripple of golden hair filled his vision.

"Oh, Amane, where are you going?"

Mahiru was in her usual clothes, so she was probably actually just on her way over to his place. It would be pretty awkward to set off now.

"Mahiru? Oh, I thought I would go for a bit of a walk. It's the last day of spring break, you know. Today's it."

"I see. You were kind of a hermit over the break, weren't you?"

"Oh, hush… A-anyway, I won't be back for a couple hours, so if you want to chill at my place, that's fine. What are you up to?"

Amane thought that his apartment had more entertainment options, so she might appreciate that, but on the other hand, she would probably feel more comfortable in her own home, so…he decided to leave it up to her.

Mahiru was staring silently up at him. Her eyes suggested that she might have something to say.

Amane wasn't sure what he was supposed to do. Nervously, he scratched his cheek. "Wh-what's up? You look like you want to come with me or something."

Amane had been about to play it off like a joke when Mahiru suddenly nodded.

"…I do."

"Eh?!"

A shrill, strangled sound spilled out from Amane's throat.

"But if you don't want me to…," Mahiru muttered, "that's fine, too, I guess."

"I-it's not that I don't you want to… It's just… How can I put this? If someone sees us together, the rumors will start up again. Aren't you worried?"

"Rumors are rumors. People are free to think whatever they want."

"G-got it," Amane replied, caught off guard by Mahiru's sudden boldness. "Well, you probably want to go get ready, so how about we leave in an hour?"

Mahiru was wearing her normal, casual clothes. She looked great just like that, but Amane figured that, being a girl, she would probably want time to change. Plus, he decided he ought to go make himself look presentable if he was going to be walking beside her. Otherwise, he would end up causing her double the trouble.

I'd better do something about my hair, he thought as he touched his bangs.

Mahiru frowned, maybe because she had realized the real reason he wanted to delay their departure. "Sorry to make you go through all that trouble for my sake..."

"Eh, don't worry about it. Besides, it'll be a good change of pace to take a walk. And I think the scenery will look nicer if you're walking with me."

It wouldn't really take too much effort to clean himself up, and it was worth it to spend time with Mahiru. He thought that she would look even more lovely than the cherry blossoms. Having a beauty like that beside him would make it all worth it, so he didn't begrudge her the extra effort.

"All right then, so I'll see you in bit?"

"O-okay."

Mahiru seemed quite reticent, but Amane just gave her a pat on the head and then ducked back into his apartment to change and work on his hairdo.

Both of them were finished getting ready after about an hour, so Amane and Mahiru set off on a leisurely walk.

Mahiru was dressed for spring. Her white dress was adorned with lace, and she wore a light-pink cardigan on top. The dress came to just above her knees, which was a little short for Mahiru, but she had on stockings, so her legs were still covered. She had even gone to the trouble of braiding her hair into a half-up style. For such a simple outing, she had certainly taken the time to compose herself, and Amane couldn't help but marvel at the beauty walking beside him.

"Is something the matter?"

"Oh, you just look very stylish today, as usual."

"...Thank you."

Mahiru's cheeks flushed slightly, and she turned away, looking every bit the innocent young damsel.

Owing to her striking appearance, Amane could feel eyes on them as they walked down the road. Mahiru didn't seem bothered by the attention, but when she looked up at him, he noticed that she was still slightly flustered. "S-so, did you have a destination in mind?"

"Well, I thought we might go down to the river and check out the cherry blossoms. I heard they've bloomed earlier than usual this year, and right now is the best time to see them."

"...Oh really?"

"So I thought I'd go take a look. Does that sound okay?"

"O-of course. I'm following you."

He felt sort of awkward, but when she gripped his sleeve tightly, all trivial thoughts vanished from his mind.

Her innocent gesture and endearing gaze made his heart leap suddenly in his chest and his breath catch in his throat.

...This is really a problem. She's way too cute.

Obviously, Mahiru was quite beautiful, but since he'd gotten to know her, Amane had only grown more infatuated. And when she touched him like that, it only intensified his feelings.

Amane brushed her delicate hand off of his sleeve and clasped his own hand around it, struggling to keep his excitement in check.

"Come on, let's go."

"Y-yeah."

It was spring break, so there were a lot of people out. As they held hands so they wouldn't lose each other, Mahiru lowered her gaze bashfully, and Amane squeezed tightly and tried to keep his cool.

When they arrived at the riverside not far from their apartment complex, the place was crowded, just like they had expected. For students, it was the final day of spring break, and for adults, it was the perfect time for a flower-viewing party. The area bustled with people sitting on tarps and blankets, enjoying the occasion.

The cherry blossoms were nearly in full bloom, and the pale petals danced before Amane's eyes.

"...Incredible! It's even better than I expected."

Amane mumbled to himself as he watched the cherry petals flutter in the breeze. He wasn't particularly interested in flowers, but he appreciated beauty when he saw it, and the delicate pink petals were undeniably beautiful.

He sighed and glanced over at Mahiru, who was staring wordlessly up at the cherry trees. The breathtaking colors were reflected in her wide eyes. Amane wondered what she was thinking.

"Mahiru?"

When he called out to her, she blinked rapidly, then turned to him in surprise. There was a strange air about her.

"What's up? You looked like you were zoning out."

"...N-nothing," Mahiru answered. "I was just... I was thinking that these really are cherry trees."

"That's because they are...," he said incredulously. "Did...did something happen? You looked sort of different, and... I dunno. I was worried."

"No, it's nothing important." Mahiru frowned. "...I just don't like...cherry blossoms...or spring very much, you know?"

"Ah, sorry, I didn't realize. I guess I shouldn't have invited you."

Amane immediately regretted taking her, but Mahiru slowly shook her head side to side.

"No, I don't mean that I hate the flowers themselves or anything... It's just, when I look at the cherry blossoms, I'm reminded that I don't have any happy memories of them."

"No happy memories?"

"Yes, because I didn't have anyone to make them with."

©Hanekoto

Mahiru smiled in a way that only made her look forlorn. She didn't seem upset. Just sad, like she had come to terms with her loneliness a long time ago. Seeing her like that put an acrid taste in Amane's mouth.

"Entrance ceremonies...and graduations, too, actually. I was alone for all of them. Miss Koyuki, the maid, didn't start her shift until the afternoon, and my parents always had more important things to do. My father would usually at least stop by to say congratulations or something, but..."

Mahiru's smile was small and bitter, and she looked up at the blossoming cherry trees. "When everyone else was holding hands with their parents under the cherry trees, I would walk home alone. And nobody was waiting for me..." Mahiru hung her head. "So you see, I don't really like spring very much. It reminds me that I don't have anyone. That probably sounds beyond pitiful..."

When Mahiru had finished, Amane couldn't help giving her hand a little squeeze. He wanted to remind her that he was still there.

There were many things that he would have liked to say to Mahiru's parents, but right now he wanted to make sure she knew that she was not alone.

"Well I'm here with you right now. I'm even holding your hand."

He stared into Mahiru's caramel-colored eyes.

She blinked dramatically, and her face twisted into a smile. "I suppose you are...," she murmured as she squeezed his hand a little tighter.

Amane gave her a reassuring smile, and with his other hand, he reached out and stroked Mahiru's hair.

"And hey, if that's not enough, I can always call Itsuki and Chitose. And my parents live pretty far away, but I'm sure if I called them, they would definitely come running..."

"I-it's fine. You don't need to do all that."

"No? All right then. Sounds like you'll just have to settle for me."

"...I'm not settling."

"Oh. Sorry, I—"

"No, that's not what I meant... I was trying to say that it's not settling, being with you."

"O-oh?"

Amane could feel a familiar heat rushing to his cheeks. He still maintained the pretense that he had no amorous intentions toward Mahiru, but hearing her tell him that she wanted him to be with her, holding her hand... It filled his stomach with butterflies.

Mahiru's expression softened into a small smile as she squeezed his hand and gazed bashfully at the falling petals. "...I think I'm starting to like the cherry blossoms, just a little bit."

Amane gently wrapped her small hand up in his.

"Is that so?"

Afterword

Thank you for picking up this book.

Since this is Volume 2, I imagine you're probably reading it after Volume 1, so thanks for coming back again. I am the author, Saekisan. Did you enjoy Volume 2 of *Angel Next Door*?

For the second book, I wanted to write a heartwarming story focused on Mahiru's feelings as she gradually comes to trust Amane. It's touching, and frustrating, and sometimes serious.

She isn't sure if she likes him, but she is certainly interested. Don't you think a heroine who is self-aware that she's starting to like someone and gets bashful about it is adorable? She really is (I say, as her doting creator).

Since I'm writing a story in which the two main characters gradually fall for each other, I plan to continue the frustration and anxiety and unintentional flirting. So look forward to that.

For the next volume, I'm (tentatively) considering having the sweet angel act a little devilish.

This is a sudden change of subject, but starting from this volume, Hanekoto has taken over full responsibility for the illustrations. I am truly grateful for Kazutake, who has been lending us his artistic talents until now.

This time, when I received Hanekoto's illustrations, I just cackled... I was simply speechless. I don't know whether I can request special favors, but I think an illustration of Mahiru borrowing one of Amane's shirts would just be the greatest. Hooray for different body sizes! Of course, all the illustrations are wonderful.

The illustration of him carrying her in his arms was a particular delight to anyone interested in size differences. The contrast between the sizes of their hands was out of this world. Of course, if I listed everything I like about the illustrations, I would run out of space, so regretfully, I must bring that to a close.

I am so happy it hurts, knowing that such wonderful illustrations will adorn my books. Thank you very much, Hanekoto. (No one can tell, but I am bowing very, very deeply.)

Well then, we've reached the end, but I'd like to give my thanks to everyone who has taken such good care of me.

To the head editors, who worked so hard to get this book published, and to everyone in the editing department at GA Novels, to the proofreader, to Hanekoto, to everyone at the printers', and to everyone who picked up a copy of this book: Truly, thank you all very much.

Let's meet again in the next volume! ...There is a next volume, right?

Thank you for reading to the very end!